The Art of Deduction

A collection of works by Sherlock Holmes fans
in support of

Save Undershaw

Compiled by Hannah Rogers
All royalties go to Help For Heroes

Edited by Steve Emecz

First edition published in 2013.
Hannah Rogers and Contributors

Paperback ISBN 9781780922348
ePub ISBN 9781780922355
PDF ISBN 9781780922362

Published in the UK by MX Publishing
335 Princess Park Manor, Royal Drive, London, N11 3GX
www.mxpublishing.co.uk

Cover design by www.staunch.com

Contents

Introduction

By Ardy of the Baker Street Babes.

www.bakerstreetbabes.com

Why Sherlock Holmes is important

Holmes himself, more often than not, wanted his name to be kept out of newspapers and public reports and was often ready to give credit for the solution to a case to the police. Yet, today, we do indeed hear of Sherlock everywhere. The stories have been adapted countless times and, according to IMDB, he has been portrayed by more actors than any other character in fiction.

The recent Warner Bros. and BBC franchises have brought scores of new people to the fandom, but even as early as the 1930s, societies devoted to the study of the Sherlock Holmes stories started to form. Indeed, Holmesians are often viewed as the "first fandom", since they invented what is termed "playing the Game": treating the Holmes stories as if Holmes, Watson and the other characters were real people, thus conflating fact and fiction, and coining their own language such as terming the collection of stories "the Canon" as though it were scripture.

So what is it that makes Holmes, Watson, and the Canon so persistently appealing to people? Here is an attempt at reconstructing some of the reasons. The stories undoubtedly have a tremendous legacy in the realm of fiction-writing, but they matter beyond that as well if we look at the characters as cultural archetypes, and, finally, on the convergence of real-life issues and the character of Holmes through the ages. Let's work our way through these.

The impact of the stories on fiction writing

The importance of the original Sherlock Holmes stories for English fiction writing cannot be overstated. Much of what we think of as modern crime fiction depends upon principles and writing devices that were employed for the first time in Sir Arthur Conan Doyle's writing of the Canon.

The collection of short stories tied together by a single main character is the most prominent of these devices. These days, it is not at all uncommon to have series of novels or short stories that all revolve around the same character(s), but the Canon is one of the first instances of short narratives that are independent of one another but feature the same main protagonist (or indeed two protagonists). Much of modern crime fiction depends on this device and is therefore heavily indebted to the Canon.

Another device is the "double act" of Holmes and Watson: dividing the protagonist into two people, one to perform the main action of detective work and one to observe, tell the story and act as point of reference and audience surrogate. The relationship, of course, is more layered and complex than this, but much of what we enjoy about "buddy cop" drama or, more generally, double acts in crime fiction, has its roots in the relationship between Holmes and Watson.

The characters as archetypes

Holmes' and Watson's relevance goes even beyond the realm of fiction. As T.S Eliot pointed out, when we talk of Holmes, we invariably fall into the fancy of his existence. From the earliest days of the publication of the stories in the Strand Magazine, people were writing letters to Holmes asking him to solve their problems.

One of the reasons why the fallacy of Holmes and Watson's existence is so prevalent is that the characters function as cultural archetypes. But not only that: their relationships as such is the prototype of the "unlikely friendship" and therefore in itself an archetype.

Taking these two considerations together, the conclusion emerges that these characters and their relationship have an essence that is universal and transcends the Victorian setting in which they were originally conceived.

Holmes is the ideal reasoner and investigator. As he puts it himself, it is his business to know what other people don't. He can solve the problems no one else can solve and many clients seek him out as a last resort after they have tried every other avenue. The cultural significance of this should become apparent if you substitute "Holmes" in the previous sentence with, say, The Doctor, Gregory House, or Cal Lightman. To watch a genius mind like that at work, we need an intermediary between him and us as an audience, which is where the Watson archetype comes in: the Doctor's Companion, James Wilson, or indeed Captain John Watson of the Fifth Northumberland Fusiliers.

We don't just adapt the stories as they are. The characters work in settings and time periods vastly different from Victorian England, and with such diverse challenges as criminal investigation, medicine, and saving the universe.

Real-life significance

Fiction, or at the least, good fiction, is always at least partly based in real life and has something significant to say about it. What significance do we take from the Canon today? Let's take a look at the BBC franchise to find some clues as to how modern people are (re-)interpreting the Canon.

Most obviously, the friendship between Holmes and Watson (or Sherlock and John) is what most resonates with audiences: two people who could not be more different from one another becoming best friends.

The BBC adaptation goes even beyond that, implying that their differences are precisely what makes their friendship work because each of them has something that the other one wants and needs. The washed-up war veteran needs a cause to fight for, the brilliant amoral reasoned needs someone to teach him compassion and the value of human life.

Less obviously, the mysteries themselves have relevance for the real lives of people. There is, in this fiction, a man who will solve the case when all hope is lost, who can see what you can't and who will repay your trust. Holmes applies logic, reason, observation and deduction and teaches us that doing the same may bring us closer to the solution of any problem or mystery we are facing.

"No one writes of Holmes and Watson without love," says John le Carré. What is more, each generation gives Holmes their problems to solve; be it Nazi spies in the Rathbones series, undiagnosable illnesses on House MD, or the mental and emotional complexities of everyday modern life on the BBC show.

Sherlock Holmes, John Watson, and the Canon matter to people on many levels, and I am sure the list of reasons could go on for longer than I have page space for. Undoubtedly, they will continue to matter for the foreseeable future, and I look forward to the next generation's take on them. But until such time may come, let's enjoy and celebrate our love for Holmes and Watson with this wonderful book, full of contributions from people all over the world, in support of the place where it all started: Undershaw House in Hindhead.

So turn the page, open the door and come in!"

The Diogenes Club

1.
The Diogenes Club by ahoy-mycroft.tumblr.com

This is a small bit on the Diogenes Club and its place in canon and in history. The idea of it has always been a bit amusing to me, and so I did a bit of research and came up with more than I'd anticipated.

There's no better way to start this out than with a quote from canon!

Holmes:
"There are many men in London, you know, who, some from shyness, some from misanthropy, have no wish for the company of their fellows. Yet they are not averse to comfortable chairs and the latest periodicals. It is for the convenience of these that the Diogenes Club was started, and it now contains the most unsociable and unclubable men in town. No member is permitted to take the least notice of any other one. Save in the Stranger's Room, no talking is, under any circumstances, allowed, and three offences, if brought to the notice of the committee, render the talker liable to expulsion. My brother was one of the founders, and I have myself found it a very soothing atmosphere."
-"The Greek Interpreter", Sir Arthur Conan Doyle

Here we get a rather innocent image of the Diogenes Club, where Sherlock explains it to be just a place for gentleman of importance could go to work or think or relax. Throughout the stories, there is no direct indication that the club is anything but what it appears to be. However, with a co-founder like Mycroft Holmes, there's got to be more.

I've had a lot of ideas about Mycroft's exact position in the British government, and from what I can see he appears to be a sort of reservoir of information:

"The conclusions of every department are passed to him, and he is the central exchange, the clearinghouse, which makes out the balance. All other men are specialists, but his specialism is omniscience."

-"The Bruce-Partington Plans", Sir Arthur Conan Doyle

I've suggested that he could work for MI6 in BBC's *Sherlock*, and what better place to collect the best minds in the British government than the Diogenes Club? Such a place would be perfect for intelligence work because it *forces* a member to be silent. They can read files and whatnot and be completely without interruption or distraction.

Holmesian scholars have also suggested that the Diogenes Club was an early form of the British intelligence community (SIS (MI6), MI5, etc), which seems logical because Mycroft, "the most indispensable man in the country" according to Sherlock, collects all governmental secrets and advises the government on what moves to make. If the Club serves that purpose, the members would have to talk, but perhaps that rule is in place just to make it appear to be an innocently-founded gentleman's club.

Even if the Club isn't the site of it all, Mycroft surely does quite a bit of his work in it since he seems to spend most of his time there, so it's still likely that the men in those armchairs have perused more than the latest periodicals.

The actual name "Diogenes" seems to come from Diogenes the Cynic, a Greek philosopher who is featured in the painting *Raphael's "School of Athens"* as the man lying across the steps. He is considered one of the founders of Cynicism, which later developed into Stoicism. He was an outcast, which seems to fit the Club fairly well.

Also, interestingly, the Diogenes Club seems to be modelled after the Athenaeum Club in Pall Mall, London. The Athenaeum is a club for high-ranking members of society (originally clergymen, now Cabinet Ministers and the like) to visit and enjoy their gigantic library and spacious rooms.

The best part is, Sir Arthur Conan Doyle himself was a member. It doesn't get much better than that.

2.

Chief by floppybelly.tumblr.com

Mycroft glowered at the front page of the morning's paper, his brother glowering back at him from under that ridiculous deerstalker. The focus of the older Holmes attention, however, was the pepper-haired Detective Inspector, with the Chief of Police hovering over him, wearing an expression not unlike Mycroft's.

The tired old government official was reminded once again of his suspicions of corruption in the higher ranks of the police. Perhaps Greg would be able to provide some insight. Mycroft looked forward to the meeting.

3.

Carnival by floppybelly.tumblr.com

Lestrade sighed and let his head sink into his hands. "First you finger the fall festival out by the forest, (Sherlock smirked at the unintentional alliteration) and now you're accusing the carnival in Surrey of being some kind of cover for a giant heroin operation? Jesus, Sherlock, not every entertainment organization has ulterior motives, just because you had one bit of trouble with that Chinese circus."

Sherlock leaned in closer, hands in his pockets. "Detective, I am positive that these two groups are part of the same network, which has been smuggling heroin, meth, and other drugs from a lab of enormous proportions in Bangkok to Britain and France." He withdrew his hand from his pocket, placing a small baggie of white powder onto Lestrade's desk.

"Please tell me that's not what I think it is," Greg deadpanned, nearly able to feel a few more of his hairs turning grey.

4.

Not a Drop of Rain in Sight by randomosityandramblings.tumblr.com

Silence weighed down upon the man as he stepped into the building; a bit restless, somewhat disheveled, and having absolutely no idea why he was here. He had just gotten out of the office when a sleek black car pulled up and the door opened, the woman inside asking him to join her. Anthea, she had called herself. Well, he supposed it wouldn't hurt and saw no way around it, so he did as told.

He hadn't predicted they'd end up here, in an elegant area filled with well-to-do gentlemen reading the paper and a silence that weighed on his shoulders, making him feel ten years older. He didn't wait long before he was shown through and into an office, the door shut behind him. He sat down in a chair facing the desk and sighed, relaxing despite himself. It had really been a long day at work. This room was at least marginally better in the way of oppressive silence, but it still felt awkward. Another five minutes passed and he was somewhat (almost) dozing off.

"My apologies, Detective Inspector. I was held up dreadfully late."
The man started and turned around, standing up on impulse; in front of him stood a well-dressed, jovial-seeming man. He was a bit more weighty than lean, with a pleasant, yet not heartfelt smile, dressed in an immaculate suit and an umbrella on his arm. He shut the door and sat down in the chair behind the desk before gesturing his guest to do the same.
"Ah, it's okay, I was just admiring—"
"No doubt you're asking yourself why I brought you here, and under such circumstances. Before I go on, I must ask you keep this a secret from Sherlock. He and I have such a—well, a strained, relationship, we'll say."
"Sherlock?"
The man shifted slightly, confusion showing so blatantly on his face a five-year-old could read it.

"My apologies. I am Mycroft Holmes, Sherlock's elder brother. I had hoped to meet the men and women my younger sibling worked so hard to belittle in a different manner, but circumstances have forced this hand."
Circumstances?
"Ah, I'm—"
"Greg Lestrade, Detective Inspector at New Scotland Yard. Yes, I know."
Mycroft gave Lestrade another of those smiles; jovial, yet slightly disdainful.

"Right, should have expected that. So what's this about?"

"Oh, just getting to know you. And I have a request."
"What's that?"
"Please, "And Mycroft leaned on his desk, elbows on it as he folded his hands in front of his mouth, "keep watching over my brother. I have many issues with him, but I do care deeply about him, and he will never accept my help."
Lestrade was somewhat unnerved by the look the man gave him, but nodded anyway. What else could he do? Obviously Mycroft was someone influential, and it was always good to stay on the good side of a Holmes.

"Excellent. Now then, I believe that you should be getting some sleep, Detective Inspector."
"Lestrade. Please, call me Lestrade." Detective Inspector sounds so formal.
Mycroft blinked for a second, observing the man over his hands, and once more Lestrade felt the analytical questioning that Sherlock had given him so many times.

"Very well. We'll be seeing each other again, I presume. Good night, Lestrade."
Lestrade stood, and nodded at Mycroft before walking out of the building and getting back in the car, telling Anthea his address. As

they drove off, he couldn't help but look at the building, wondering just what he had gotten himself into. Mycroft seemed harmless enough. But he was a Holmes, and there was always more than meets the eye.

Lestrade shook his head, got out and headed into his flat, settling down on the couch and rubbing his eyes. He'd dwell on the absurdities of the people he worked with later. Right now he was going to sleep, dwelling on the question of why someone would carry an umbrella when there wasn't a drop of rain in sight.

5.

Acquiring a Consulting Detective by white-fang.tumblr.com

The first time Gregory Lestrade meets Sherlock, there are no murders, or kidnappings, or lunatic bombers--in fact, none of the things that Greg will come to almost automatically associate with Sherlock in a few years. Greg is only a detective sergeant, and Anderson hasn't even come into the picture yet.

No, it's the cocaine. Of course it's the cocaine.

Greg hates seeing lives consumed by drugs, hates it more when they're young. Male, nineteen, and the tiny, neat puncture marks on the inside of both elbows tell Greg far more than he wants to know.

"Sherlock Holmes," he reads off the top of the file, shaping carefully the unfamiliar name. "Possession of cocaine, a Class A substance. Do you have anything you want to say about that?"

"What's there to say?" The reply is sharp, petulant. "It seems a simple enough conclusion. So is the fact that your wife is having an affair."

"That's not--what?" Greg hadn't confided in anyone of his suspicions--had almost convinced himself that he was just being paranoid. "Who told you that?"

"Your deodorant and your cuffs." The boy's blue-grey eyes are slightly unfocused, but no less cutting for that. "Detective Sergeant, how have you not noticed? The standards in this place are slipping--if there were any to begin with."

Greg fights his rapidly growing annoyance, because it would be unprofessional to yell at this boy, so scrawny as to consist entirely of corners. "Look," he says finally, managing to sound merely irritated instead of murderous, "I am trying to help you."

That only earns him a disbelieving sneer. "You're a police officer. Your job is to find and catch criminals, not to help people." The last two words are spat out with an alarming vehemence. "Well, you've caught me. So why don't you lock me up and wash your hands free of the whole affair?" The boy leans back in his chair, a study in nonchalance.

Except...despite the slight, Greg is a good police officer. And there's something in that lifted chin, the deliberately open posture that tells him that Sherlock is scared.
No matter how defiant Sherlock is, he's still so very young.
"And are you?" Greg asks, softly, calmly. It's quite like trying to tame a wild animal.
"Am I what?"
"A criminal."
Sherlock snaps shut like a trap. "That's not a standard question," he says stiffly. "And you can't possibly expect to get an objective answer."
"You don't understand what I expect." Greg stands up. "I'm going to let you off with a caution."
"A caution?" An eyebrow, raised in disdain. "Bad policy. No wonder the crime rates are so high around here."
Behind Greg's eyes, a headache is slowly forming. "Stop talking before I change my mind." He hands off Sherlock to a passing constable with more than a little relief. But as the black-haired boy is escorted down the hall, Greg can't help but try one more time. "Sherlock!" he calls. "I don't want to see you in here again, you hear me?"
A brief shrug is all he receives for his troubles. Sherlock doesn't even turn around.

Four months later, Sherlock is sitting in front of Greg again. This time, he's somehow managed to acquire a black eye.
"Who did that?" Greg nods at the injury, feeling inexplicably outraged.
"It's not important."
"Just answer me."
But Sherlock doesn't, only sits there taking quick, shallow breaths while the bruise darkens. He looks even skinnier than before, fragile and just a little bit lost. "You've moved out," he says suddenly.
"I--what?"

"Did you finally confront your wife? You've wanted to for a while. But no, you wouldn't do something like that, not without--oh."
"What are you on about?" Unfortunately, Greg thinks Sherlock already knows the answer.
"You found them together, didn't you? But you moved out, not your wife." Sherlock cocks his head to the side and scrutinises Greg thoughtfully. "I see," he declares after a moment. "You're too kind, sergeant. If she loved the children that much, she wouldn't have had the affair."
"Shut up!" Greg finally loses hold on his fraying temper. "First of all, this is none of your business. Second, I'll be the one asking questions. Was it cocaine again?"
"Haven't read the report? No, it was heroin."
The way he drops the name so casually--as if they're talking about what Sherlock had for breakfast instead of what dangerous drug is running through his bloodstream--is infuriating. "Fine," Greg says tightly. "I'll have someone take you to lock-up."
It occurs to Greg, much, much later that Sherlock had looked almost happy as he rattled off his conclusions.

Mycroft Holmes.
Greg hadn't even known that Sherlock had a brother, let alone one who dressed in tailored suits and wielded an umbrella like a sword.
"Hello, Detective Sergeant," says the man, all careful smiles that aren't smiles at all. "I understand that you've taken Sherlock into custody."
"Did someone contact you?" Greg frowns. "Sherlock didn't mention anyone at all."
"No, of course he wouldn't have. I'm afraid he's always been a bit too...wild for his own good." Mycroft's rueful tone is pitched just right to invite sympathy.
Greg doesn't give it.
The man sighs, and when he next speaks his voice is much more authoritative. "I'll be taking my brother with me. Please don't feel the need to file a report; it won't be necessary."

"That's against regulations," Greg points out.
"Is it?" A mild question, but it makes Greg's spine stiffen all the same. "I'll have the requisite paperwork sent over."
The next morning, there are orders from high, and no evidence that one Sherlock Holmes has ever been arrested for possession of heroin.
The Holmes brothers are going to drive Greg mad.

When the two of them meet for the third time, seven years later, Greg has been promoted, and Sherlock comes in voluntarily.
"Detective Inspector Lestrade," he says, sweeping into the office like small whirlwind, "I need a look at the murder victim."
"What murder victim? And who let you in here?"
Sherlock waves away the second question with a vague gesture. "Let me examine Alison Hewitt."
"That case has been ruled a suicide. And how do you know about it, anyway?"
"No, no, it can't possibly have been suicide. Look at the teaspoon!"
"What teaspoon?"
"Exactly! The sugar bowl's out, tea-tray's neatly arranged, but there's no sign of the teaspoon. "
"What's that got to do with anything?"
The look Sherlock sends in response is pure contempt. "If Alison Hewitt had actually poisoned her own tea and before drinking it, why would she have felt the need to hide the teaspoon? It's obvious that someone else poisoned the tea, then took the teaspoon. Perhaps to hide the fingerprints, perhaps for another reason. She drank the tea, though, so she either trusted the poisoner or chose to be poisoned. I need to see the body to conclude one way or the other."
"I can't just let you investigate this. You're not even qualified--"
At that Sherlock's eyes flash darkly. "You've moved back in with your wife," he starts, "but you're using separate bedrooms. Trust issues? Possibly. One of your children--daughter, I would guess--has recently been sick. A man named Anderson might be

transferred to your forensics team, but you're not sure if he's right for the job. He's not, by the way--I've already spoken with him. You have an unsolved murder on your hands, and I'm more qualified than anyone in this building. Now, are you going to let me see her or not?"
"You should really stop talking about my family," Greg says wearily.
"Not the point."
With a sigh, Greg Lestrade makes a decision that will change his life. "Are you clean?" he asks.
"Yes. For five years now." Sherlock smiles, and the expression is sharp, pure.
"Three minutes, and then I want you out."
As Sherlock bounds out of the room, Greg wonders if he's just imagining the muffled "Thank you."

And so New Scotland Yard acquires a consulting detective.

6.

Pirates & Spies by Mira Frenzel

Sherlock Holmes, seven years old, jumped down from the shelf on which he was not meant to be climbing.

"Avast, ye scurvy dogs! Captain Sherlock, scourge of the seven seas has arrived in port! Give me all your booty!" He was brandishing his cardboard sword, tricorn hat jauntily placed on his head. His older brother rolled his eyes, and without even looking up from his book, pointed his umbrella at Sherlock.

"Bang. There. I've shot you with my umbrella-gun."

"That's not right, Mycroft. They didn't have spies with secret guns when there were pirates."

"I think you'll find that they did."

Sherlock stamped his foot. "But not like spies spies. Not like John Steed."

"To be fair, the modern portrayals of both spies and pirates are horribly romanticized." Mycroft sat up and slid a thin strip of paper in his book.

"Well, I can be a pirate if I want to." Sherlock crossed his arms.

"Then I shall be a spy." Mycroft smiled a little as he suddenly charged for the younger Holmes, who ran off giggling. Mycroft was starting to enjoy himself, and he hid behind a curtain. He heard the sound of Sherlock's little bare feet padding across the hardwood flooring, slowing down as he realized Mycroft was nowhere in sight, and then speeding up again as he made for the curtain. Mycroft felt the jab of the cardboard sword into his stomach and heard a cry of "Aha! Take that, you government scum!"

Mycroft's plan was in place and he outstretched his arms to trap Sherlock in the curtain. "And now you'll tell us where you've hidden the cache of microdots!"

"Never," came a muffled cry of playful defiance.

"I have ways of making you talk, Captain Sherlock!" He knew exactly where Sherlock was ticklish and instantly started tickling him.

"I've faced hordes of—" Sherlock couldn't get out his statement about having faced death time and time again at the hands of oppressive governments. "Mycr—"

"Where have you hidden the microdots?" Mycroft was smiling now, a broad grin on his face.

Sherlock's giggles were punctuated by statements of defiance and the odd pirate grunt. "I'll never tell you!"

Their mother stuck their head around the corner. "It's time for dinner—what are you doing?"

"Punghfts nd spughs!"

"Pirates and spies, apparently." Mycroft stood up and took the curtains off his younger brother. Sherlock was bright red in the face and his hat had fallen off. He put it back on his head.

"It's in the shipwreck lagoon," he said as a parting shot before running to dinner.

7.
Ten Tears by Dezmin Humphryis

The first time Lestrade cried as an adult was when he had his first kiss.

At twenty, he had given up hopes of ever having a girlfriend and experiencing the electric charge of a first kiss people always talked about. He knew he was straight, he was an avid rugby player, drank pint after pint of beer at parties, and had a, large, collection of magazines full of half naked women. His sexuality was never questioned by others. But for some reason he was never able to obtain a girlfriend.

'Sorry, we're just friends, Greg.'

'You're sweet, but not my type, Greg.'

'I love you, just not like that, Greg.'

Lestrade thought that time would fix it. He would find the right girl eventually. But as time wore on he started to get desperate. He'd plead, beg, confess his love, until eventually he came to the conclusion something was wrong with him.

He'd be single forever.

So when Jessica, a fellow police recruit, asked him out one day in the cafeteria, Lestrade couldn't believe it. It wasn't until they were at the movies that night, her head on his shoulder and their fingers laced together, that the fact that he had a girlfriend, he was no longer single, dawned on him.

And he couldn't believe the curse had lifted.

He was determined to make the night romantic, everything a girl would want in a date. He brought her snacks, offered his jacket when she shivered, and walked her up to her dorm door when they arrived back.

He was about to say goodnight and leave when Jessica leant forward and offered him something he never thought any girl would give him.

It was clumsy and awkward. Lestrade knew too much theory and had no practical experience to make it romantic. Their noses

squished together, lips were wet and slimy, and his tongue too big for her mouth.
It wasn't what he imagined. It was completely different and even more intense. He couldn't help the tears that welled.
He apologized again and again to her. For the awkward kiss, for crying, for apologizing. She had told him it was okay, that it happened a lot, and held him close while he continued to wipe tears from his eyes.
She had lied.
The next day Lestrade was single. Not that he really minded. He had finally tasted the forbidden fruit and it would keep him well fed for some time.

*****

The second time Lestrade cried as an adult was six years later, at his wedding.
He couldn't help it, after three years of dating he was finally marrying the love of his life, Kirstie. He had no involvement in planning the wedding, he was too busy with his work, besides, Kirstie had wanted a wedding since she was a little girl so it was her day and she was going to have it exactly how she wanted.
Not that Lestrade minded, he knew the day was hers and was speechless at everything she had done. The church was old and small, but she had decorated it in whites and reds to give the illusion of space, roses were everywhere, and candles filled the church with a pleasant scent. Lestrade appreciated the hard work behind this beauty.
He wasn't prepared for the beauty of his bride, however.
To him she was an angel. It was cliché, but when he saw her walking down the aisle, dressed in white, with the sun shining on her hair like a halo, it was the only way he knew how to describe her. As she got closer he started to cry and couldn't stop. The entire ceremony he cried and grinned like an idiot.
Later, during the reception, his friends and her father would make jokes about his tears.
'You cried more than the bride.'

'I've never seen the groom get so worked up at a wedding.'
'Are you sure you're marrying a man?'

But Lestrade didn't care, he let the comments slide off his back, they didn't faze him. That day, he was the happiest he felt in his entire life.

*****

Greg Lestrade is a man. A man's man he likes to think. And a man's man does not cry. Of course, Lestrade rationalizes, there are certain exceptions.
The birth of his first child is one of those exceptions.
It had been a long labour, thirty-four hours, most of which Lestrade spent waiting, worrying, panicking, in the sitting room. Several of his colleagues had come and gone, their congratulations short as they went back to work, some of their family came, but most had left after they realized just how long a birth could take. Only their parents remained until the end.
Finally, with much relief, a nurse came out to announce that a healthy baby girl had been born. Her parents were the first to see it, Lestrade had been too nervous to even move from his seat. He had sent his parents in next as he tried to calm his nerves.

An hour after his daughter was born, Lestrade finally went in to see her. Everyone had left, and his wife had drifted off to sleep, the room was quiet apart from little gurgles his daughter made. At first he was unsure of what to do, the little, chubby human stared up at him as he stared back at her. Then, finally, he picked her up and held her.
The tears were sudden and silent. He couldn't, didn't want to, control them. His baby daughter smiled up at him and he knew that, for as long as he lived, no matter what she did, how many parties she snuck out for, or boys she dated, he would always, love her.
'My little Melissa.'

*****

Melissa was the source of more tears for Lestrade.
Her first day at school was an emotional time. The weeks beforehand Lestrade had been busy with work, which meant Kirstie had been the one to organize enrolments and buy school supplies.
So when Lestrade woke one morning to find his little girl, hair up in pigtails and pack on her back, excited about her first day at school, it came as a complete surprise.
He watched, shocked, as Melissa ran around the kitchen and sang about how she was a big girl going to school. Eventually Kirstie caught the five-year old and announced it was time to go. Lestrade hugged his daughter as tight as he could before she squirmed and slipped away, a grin on her face.
He watched through the window as Kirstie's car drove away, taking his little girl to school. Then the realization hit him. His baby girl was growing up. He had missed so much of his daughter's life, because of work, and suddenly she was going off to school. Soon she would be off to high school, he thought, then college, and then she'd be married and have children of her own.
He didn't know why he cried, didn't know if it was joy or regret, but he couldn't stop the tears either way. Eventually, when he realized he was be late, he wiped his face and, with the smile of a proud father, left for work.

*****

The next time Lestrade cried was at his father's funeral.
His death was sudden and unexpected. A stroke. His family was devastated and Lestrade forced himself to be strong, to be there for everyone, and to handle all the arrangements. For five days he comforted his devastated mother, called funeral home after funeral home, collected photos from family and friends, and picked out a plot.
So when the day of the funeral came, it became too much. The sky was a bright, the sun shone, and birds sang happily. The day only emphasized how much Lestrade hurt. He hated it. Everyone

gathered in the church and cried as they watched the video Lestrade had put together to highlight his father's life.
'He was a great man.'
'He led a full and joyful life.'
'He will be missed by all of us here and many more.'
But Lestrade wouldn't cry yet. He had seen the video, rehearsed the speech, over and over again, he could keep himself together through them.
He held his mother's hand as the funeral progression made its way out of the church and towards the graveyard. She sobbed into his arm as he watched his father's body lower into the ground.
Then he began to cry.
Breathless, heaving, sobs wracked their way from Lestrade's throat. He couldn't breathe, but couldn't stop crying. It seemed endless. Kirstie tried to comfort him, but she couldn't stop the tears.
Later he calmed down. The tears dried up and the sobs ceased. He no longer cried but the grief had not left.

*****

If questioned about the next time he cried, Lestrade will swear that he was not crying. It was allergies.
Lestrade wasn't interested in the politics that plagued the Yard. He became a police officer to protect the innocent, not to put his fingers in anyone's pies, or work his way up the ladder. He simply wanted to do his job, and he did his job well.
So when the previous Detective Inspector resigned after some scandalous information was leaked within the Yard, Lestrade wasn't a real candidate for the position.
Not that he was interested. Yes, he daydreamed about the money, about how he could do a better job, but he didn't want to get involved in the backstabbing politics several others who wanted the position were in.
No one expected Lestrade to get the promotion, especially himself. So when he was called in to receive the news, he was speechless and didn't understand why he was being promoted to the position.

'You've one of the highest arrest records we've seen in a long time.'
'You're spoken very highly of, by the man who nominated you, and all your colleagues.'
'You've great morals, Lestrade, morals that are needed in this position.'
Lestrade didn't speak throughout the entire exchange, just stared, in disbelief, as he was congratulated and told what was expected of him as the new detective inspector.
Word spread quickly throughout the Yard and it seemed that everyone wanted to congratulate him. His hand began to tingle from all the handshakes, his back hurt from all the slaps, and his eyes began to water from,
'Sorry, my allergies are acting up.'
No one believed his excuse, no matter how insistent he was, but they didn't question it, the man had been promoted, he was allowed to cry.

*****

Lestrade will admit, with a faint blush to his cheeks, that the next time he cried as an adult was for the birth of his second child.
Nine months after his promotion, his wife went into labour at nine A.M. He had been flooded with paperwork, a 'perk' they never told him came with the new position, and wasn't able to go into the hospital straight away.
'It's okay, Greg, I'll still be here when you finish.'
'Relax, remember how long Melissa took?'
'Stay at work, I'll be fine.'
He managed to get out of work at nine P.M, by which time his son was already sixty-three minutes old. He was ninety-seven minutes old by the time Lestrade managed to get into the hospital and to his wife's room.

Tears welled as soon as he saw his son.
'Oh god, I'm so sorry.'
'Are you alright? Is he alright?'
'I'm so sorry.'

Lestrade's apologies were accepted and he was told that their baby boy perfectly healthy, if not a little bit fat compared to his sister. He slept soundly in his mother's arms and didn't even stir when Lestrade held him.

All the feelings he had the first time he held Melissa came flooding back. Lestrade smiled as tears ran down his cheeks, he didn't notice them until one fell. He didn't try to explain them away, he knew he couldn't anyway, so he continued to smile at his sleeping son while the tears continued to fall.

*****

It was another four years before Lestrade cried again.
A murder of a woman took him to a house ten minutes away from his own home. Usually, he would spend the entire day at crime scenes and the Yard, but, as he was only a stone's throw away, he figured he'd stop by home for lunch.
Later, upon reflection, he would curse himself for not seeing the, 'obvious', signs Sherlock had informed him of. But at that moment he had no real reason to be suspicious as he pulled up in his driveway.
The house was quiet. Not silent, the TV in the living room was on and next door must have been hammering because there was a constant 'thump thump'. But it didn't have the usual noise a house with a four year old should have.
Lestrade began searching the house for his elusive son. Not in the living room, not in the kitchen, not out in the backyard, no where downstairs. He began the search upstairs, meanwhile the thumping was getting louder and he could hear voices through the walls.
That was when his stomach began to twist, he approached his own bedroom and it was clear the thumping wasn't the neighbour and the voices were just beyond the door. He stared at the chipped wood, trying to decide what to do. His hand hovered above the handle, unsure whether he should continue, or simply go back to work.

He didn't get to decide.
He knew the man that opened the door. He knew him, but he couldn't place where. They stared at each other, both in shock, until Kirstie cried out in surprise and began to babble excuses. The man didn't get a chance to speak before Lestrade punched him in the face and kicked him, naked, out of the house.
Kirstie's apologetic excuses quickly turned into angry reasons when it became clear Lestrade didn't believe her.
'You're never here, always at work!'
'We haven't touched each other in forever!'
'I don't love you anymore, Greg!'
Her words didn't reach him, his mind was reeling, he felt sick. He couldn't believe what had just happened, couldn't believe Kirstie, his wife and love of his life, would cheat on him. He left the house, got in his car, and drove back to work.
The numbness he had felt for the last twenty minutes faded and the realization of the situation sank in. He pulled into his parking spot, turned off the engine, and stared at the dirty, blank, concrete wall.
His hands shook first, then his shoulders began to shake, and then his chest heaved with great, silent breaths. He knew he was late, that he'd be reprimanded later, but at that moment he couldn't control himself.
In his car, in a silent parking lot, Greg Lestrade held his head in his hands and sobbed.

*****

Lestrade and Kirstie were unable to work out their problems.
They had tried, well he had tried, but she continued to have the affair with their daughter's P.E teacher. A math or English teacher Lestrade might have been able to handle, but P.E teachers weren't really teachers.
And so, after eighteen months of separation, their divorce was almost over. All that was left was the custody of the children.

Lestrade had one of the best lawyers from the D.A's office, a mate that owed him a favour, and they were confident that the custody would be granted to both parents.
Kirstie was fighting for full custody...
And whatever Kirstie wanted, Kirstie got.
Lestrade couldn't believe the judge as the ruling was passed. He didn't feel his legs underneath him as he realized he could no longer see his kids without a pre-arranged meeting. He swore at the judge, at his ex-wife, at his lawyer, until he was threatened with jail time.
John Watson found him later, drinking in a dank pub. He didn't speak, just sat beside his friend and waited...
'Full custody! Can you believe it?!'
'I've a well respected job, I can provide for them.'
'Unstable work hours, they said. I was never home, she said.'
'Yeah? Well it's fucking sexist! I love my kids, it's that bitch that-'
The words got caught in his suddenly too tight throat and he pressed the heel of his hands into his eyes, ashamed, exhausted, and in mourning over those important moments he was to lose in his kids' lives.
John didn't offer condolences right away, just rested a hand on Lestrade's shoulder as it shook with grief.

*****

The next time Lestrade cried, he didn't try to hide it.
He had known Sherlock for years, and had worked with him for longer. He knew his mind worked differently, knew he saw what people didn't, knew he truly was a genius. No matter what those around him said, no matter how much they didn't believe, Lestrade knew, Lestrade believed, and that was all that mattered to him.
The papers after Sherlock's death made him sick, he couldn't bear to look at them. Not just because they called a great, no, a good man, a liar and a fake, but because it made him remember the doubt he felt about Sherlock's innocence.

The funeral was tiny, almost non-existent, especially compared to Lestrade's father's. There was no video showing the highlights of Sherlock's life, only a few bouquets of daisies Mrs. Hudson had brought decorated the grave, and less than ten people were present.
Lestrade didn't think the few reporters counted.

Mrs. Hudson and Molly cried, and John stared at the grave. It was a look Lestrade had seen many times before, at colleagues' funerals, at victims' funerals, he was sure he had had it at his father's funeral. It was the look of anger and loss while he tried not to let his emotions show. John was a soldier after all.

The silence, the grief, became too much. Lestrade cleared his throat, lowered his head, and spoke.

'When I first met you, I wanted to punch you. Actually, I did punch you.'
'You were a good man, you saved many lives. It doesn't matter how much of a prick you were, that fact will never change.'
'We'll miss you, Sherlock.'

He couldn't continue, he could only stand there, staring at the grave, as he wept over his lost friend.

11.

Diogenes Club by floppybelly.tumblr.com

Mycroft sighed (silently) and crossed his legs, carefully folding his newspaper to the next page. The one other occupant in the room politely ignored him. Mycroft knew the reason for the club's recent drop in attendance rates. Ever since he'd gotten more involved in the lives of his brother (and by extension, his brother's associates), the club had been paid numerous visits by non-members who simply didn't understand. Mycroft had tried explaining things to John upon his second visit to the club.

"It's an establishment for persons with a need for companionable solitude," Mycroft had said over the tips of his fingers, hunched over his desk in his personal office.

"You... DO know that's a contradiction, right?" John had squinted at the government official, one eyebrow quirked in confusion.

"You should be more than familiar with the contradictory nature which resides about many factors of my life." Mycroft knew he wouldn't have to go into detail for his brother's companion to understand.

However, the loud interruptions which forced the members of the club out of their precious headspace became more numerous as the days passed. First it was just John, then when he would admit to needing his official assistance, Sherlock; eventually their antics bled over until even the poor Detective Inspector became involved, and that had been the final straw.

Nowadays, the club was emptier than it had ever been, though you wouldn't know by listening. Mycroft let a slight sigh of loneliness escape his lips, and the room's one other occupant stood and left.

12.

Lestrade by floppybelly.tumblr.com

Greg stepped out of his doorstep for what would probably be the last time in a long while. A world-heavy sigh made his head hang as a light mist enveloped the city, shrouding him in with it as though he'd always been there, on his stoop, looking as though he had nowhere left in the world to go.

"You're practically married to your work anyway," she'd told him, handing him his case full of suits and spare badges and toiletries and his grandmother's watch, "You might as well go on and live very happily together. Just don't expect to come crawling back here for any sympathy."

The Detective Inspector had become nearly a permanent fixture in the Yard as of late, always wrapped up in these cases which seemed to escalate in difficulty and intensity and... pure grotesque, poetic horror, really. It had taken a toll on his already-strained relationship with his soon-to-be-ex wife. Tonight had been the final straw, when Greg had brought his work home with him again.

Lestrade caught a cab to the Yard. It wouldn't be the first night he'd slept in his office chair.

13.
Cake by Amanda Dotterer

It was a rainy day in London, but it had recently slowed down to a drizzle. It was also a Sunday, which meant Mycroft Holmes would be going out to another restraint with his father. He had already put on his best clothes, shoes, and jacket. The eager eleven year old stood on the front porch with his umbrella, looking up and down the street for his father's car. After ten minutes, Mycroft checked his watch to make sure he wasn't early to find what he already knew -- his father was late. A thousand possibilities as to why ran through his head. Maybe there was traffic on the roads. Maybe he had been the victim of a crime.

But been those ideas were unlikely. Unless he had been the victim of a crime, he would have called, and even then, the police would have called to tell them.

Mycroft sighed and folded his umbrella, leaning on it instead. It took a half an hour before his mother called him back inside to tell him that his father wasn't coming to get him. Ever.

xxx

Twenty years later, Mycroft sat on the couch in his sitting room. He was no longer the excited boy who had waited for his father on the steps. He went either alone or with his husband to the restraints he and his father used to frequent, but spent most of his time working. (Being the British government wasn't as easy as it looked.) Although Mycroft had tried to learn how to cook, it upset him more than it helped him. His husband was an excellent cook, though, and made wonderful desserts.

Despite having already had a slice of cake, Mycroft decided that he would have another. One for his father.

14.
A Quiet Birthday by Alice Maher

Mycroft Holmes viewed birthdays with a kind of good-humoured cynicism. It wasn't that he disliked the idea of ageing; it was pointless to waste energy worrying over something so inevitable. But he did dislike the inane and repetitive 'well-wishing' that seemed to dominate the occasion. Holding a small position in the British government meant that there were a great many individuals that felt the need to stroke their own sense of importance by sending him the obligatorily-horrendous birthday card, with a few hastily-written lines that he never bothered to read. No, if a birthday were to be cause for celebration, he liked to do so on his own terms: alone.

Hence it had become a personal tradition over the years to spend the majority of the day at his beloved Diogenes Club. If other attendees were even aware of the date's significance, they never felt the need to inform him. After all, the club played host to some of the most anti-social gentlemen of London, and the policy of total silence meant that it was not a place that one went looking for conversation. Mycroft would sit in his favourite chair and indulge in a slice of coffee cake from the tea tray, as he pored over his many papers. And for many years his birthday had passed in this comfortably unremarkable fashion. It was one of the many advantages to having no living relatives, save for an estranged brother whose concept of social norms was usually even more skewed than his own.

But then fate had intervened in the form of a maternal landlady and an ex-army doctor who had proven to be quite a curious influence on said brother. The changes in Sherlock Holmes were initially quite subtle; he looked better-fed, though he still retained that effortlessly-lean physique that Mycroft had always resented. He laughed more often, but less at other people's expense (though there were some notable exceptions to that rule). All in all, he was acting more human than his older brother had ever seen him. It came as part-relief, part worry for Holmes-the-elder that the young detective had chosen to place such trust in other people.

On the one hand, it eased the self-appointed burden of responsibility somewhat, when there were others keeping track of the man's habits and watching out for danger nights. But there was also the nagging concern that people were unreliable, sentimental and general liabilities to people like Sherlock Holmes, who unwisely gave his full energy to anything (or anyone) he deemed important enough. Part of it, a part far bigger than Mycroft really liked to admit, was disappointment that when the man had finally decided to let others back into that 'funny little head' of his, it was not to his only family that he had turned. John Watson's presence helped soften the hostility Sherlock had been directing at his brother ever since that dreadful business all those years ago, but he knew they would never again be considered 'close.'

Hence it came as something of a surprise when his birthday solitude was interrupted by the arrival of Sherlock Holmes to the Diogenes Club, carrying a violin case in one hand and wearing a carefully-blank expression. Mycroft rose from his seat the instant his brother crossed the threshold, expecting some great emergency to have sent him so unexpectedly to the clubhouse he usually made a point of avoiding. But he waved away the silent signal toward the Stranger's Room, (where they would be permitted to discuss any problem aloud) instead gesturing for Mycroft to resume his seat.

Perplexed, Mycroft watched as Sherlock drew up his own chair and sat down, case resting on his lap. The detective refused to meet his eye at first, instead occupying himself with a detailed observation of the small oak-panelled room and its occupants. Mycroft remained unconvinced that there wasn't some terrible reason for this abrupt arrival, but consigned himself to the fact that whatever the issue was, it clearly wasn't too pressing. Indeed, Sherlock looked prepared to spend quite a while at the club. He had removed his gloves and tucked them into his coat pocket, and was slouched in a perfect imitation of the most languid members. He finally met Mycroft's questioning stare and raised his brows defiantly, daring him to protest his presence.

Mycroft shrugged. He had far too much composure to appear ruffled by such a development. If Sherlock Holmes was there to test his patience, then he would leave disappointed. He picked up a dainty silver fork and carefully cut his slice of coffee cake in half. Moving the larger piece onto another plate, he handed it to his brother with a great show of courtesy. An outside observer might not have realised the subtle power-play and unspoken words that were passing between the pair as they sat and enjoyed the silence. Roughly translated, their body language said something along the lines of:
"I thought you were meant to be on a diet?"

"It's my birthday. Cake is traditional birthday fare, and therefore perfectly allowable today."
"Hmm, *Heaven forbid* Mycroft Holmes ignore *tradition.*"
"I didn't have to offer you any, you know."
"Actually, this is quite good. From the organic bakery on Kingston Lane, judging by the icing."
Sherlock finished the whole piece without the slightest protest, knowing it would annoy Mycroft to see him so agreeable. Usually the young man would have complained about the mental energy being wasted on something as pointless as digestion, and criticised his brother's love for those things that he considered little more than 'transport.' Yes, he was definitely up to something; Mycroft hadn't seen Sherlock in such a curious mood since the day he'd been escorted to Buckingham Palace wearing nothing but a sheet. He was almost... playful. The older Holmes fought the urge to roll his eyes as he returned to his mountain of paperwork.
Squeak.

The first, tremulous note of a violin being tuned cut through the silence like a gunshot. Several heads turned to look in the direction of the intrusion, expressions ranging from curious to openly antagonistic. Mycroft's eyes widened in horror. Naturally he had been suspicious of the violin case ever since his brother's arrival, but he had never allowed himself to believe Sherlock would *actually* do something as scandalous as play music in the mute club. Sherlock, to his brother's heightened fury, paid the onlookers no heed. Each experimental pluck of the strings was like a crack spreading through a sheet of glass; eventually the whole thing would shatter.

Finally satisfied, Sherlock tucked the instrument beneath his chin and took up his bow. He paused just before it touched the strings, waiting to see what his brother would do. Mycroft, a man who prided himself on having a solution to every problem, found himself yet again stymied by the young upstart's reckless nature. There was nothing he could do save from leaping across the tea tray and seizing the damned thing himself, and he didn't think even *his* natural dignity would survive such a display. Hands balled into fists of impotent fury, he could only watch on as his brother, grinning wickedly, began to play.

Happy birthday to you, happy birthday to you...

The tune was unmistakeable. It filled the room with its indecently-cheerful melody, causing the onlookers to smirk. It was Mycroft Holmes' birthday, and his brother was giving him the gift of music; whether he accepted it or not. Pinching the bridge of his nose in exasperation, the stoic government official stared down at his work documents and willed it all to be over. Finally, with a dramatic flourish, Sherlock returned the violin to its case and silenced reigned in The Diogenes Club once more.

Mycroft Holmes could give a cabinet minister a nervous breakdown or make a criminal beg for life imprisonment. But even his most sinister glare had no effect on his little brother, who met it with his usual boldfaced impudence. Gritting his teeth, Mycroft picked up an expensive-looking pen and drew a question mark on the corner of one of his papers. He underlined it twice and turned it to face Sherlock. The corner of the detective's mouth twitched in amusement at the new method of communication. He scribbled a reply in his own Moleskine notebook, tore out the page and folded it in half, like a card. Placing it on the tea-tray, he gave one last nod to his brother, picked up his violin case and strolled out into the street. As the front door snapped shut, Mycroft could have sworn he heard him laugh.

~*~

Mycroft Holmes viewed birthdays with a kind of wistful sadness. It wasn't that he missed his youth; memories were often far sweeter than the reality. But he did miss the little brother from his youth, the curly-headed boy who played pirate and begged Mycroft to draw him treasure maps of the backyard. He missed the man he had grown into, the self-proclaimed Consulting Detective who ran around London solving crimes and getting in and out of trouble. How sorely he missed that man, who knew caring wasn't an advantage but had gone and done it anyway.

Sitting in the same chair in the same club on the same day as last year, Mycroft read his papers and ate his cake in silence. There was nobody to interrupt him with their well-wishing, nobody to break the solitude with their noise. Once again his birthday was a quiet one. But it was not as peaceful as it had once seemed. He was restless, expecting someone that would never arrive. Listening for music that would never be played. There was an old slip of paper weighing down his front pocket and every so often he had to take it out and look at it again, if only to remind himself that it existed. It was a torn piece of notepaper, folded in half like a card. And on the inside were three simple words in a familiar hand:

HAPPY BIRTHDAY, MYCROFT.

Pictures in order.

1. Diogenes & Scotland Yard by oneoftheexactsciences.tumblr.com
2. Gregory Lestrade by inklou.tumblr.com
3. Lestrade by draloreshimare.deviantart.com
4. Lestrade by Sophie Charalampopoulou
5. Mycroft's First Love by kazujun.tumblr.com

OGENES CLUB
NEW SCOTLAND YARD
TOP SECRET
Diet? SH
Case? SH

OH CAKE YOU ARE SO FUNNY
kazujm.tumblr

We Believe In Sherlock Holmes

1.

Disseminate by floppybelly.tumblr.com

In the weeks that had followed the dismissive (and false) news reports, John had dealt with his pain in a method which was both private and public at the same time. Taking up a disguise, a respirator, and a can of yellow paint, he had done his best to disseminate the #believeinsherlock propaganda throughout the entire city, covering the skate parks and abandoned power plants, and as he grew bolder and angrier, the tube stops and the sides of buildings, until finally he found himself running away from a fresh stencil on the side of Kitty Riley's corporate office building.

The most astonishing thing John had found, apart from the level of sheer exhilaration the tagging brought to him, had been when his yellow paint had been joined by the signatures and slogans of others. His #believeinsherlock now went hand in hand with a red #moriartywasreal, and eventually, a green #trustyourinstincts. (John had had to look that one up, to make sure it was part of his war) (Was it a war?) The campaign was slowly growing to an infectious scale, and John could relish the looks he caught from passersby as he saw them tilt their heads in puzzlement at the odd graffiti, or nod slightly in agreement as they passed by. Nobody seemed to react in a disagreeable way, and it made John's heart soar that Moriarty's final plan had not been entirely successful.

2.
This is the Movement of the Century' by Katie Volker

Dr. John Watson stared at the words on the wall in amazement. He touched the paint. Yellow, exact same as the one used in The Blind Banker case. It was also still wet. He looked about the alleyway, but there was no one there. He picked up his shopping and continued walking back to his flat.

He'd moved out of Baker Street. It was too hard for him to stay there now. Too many memories. He did stop by every so often to check on Mrs Hudson. They have tea and biscuits. Mrs Hudson would always try to get him to talk about Sherlock, but John would always change the subject. He lived with Stamford now, grudgingly. Mycroft and Lestrade had ganged up on him a few months after Sherlock's death, forcing him to get up and do something. He'd spiralled for a while. Little too much alcohol for one man. He was in hospital for three weeks.

As he walked home, a poster caught his eye. When he saw the picture, he nearly dropped his bags and ran. On the poster was Moriarty's face with the caption:

Richard Brook= FRAUD. Moriarty was REAL.

He gazed at it, feeling happy, touched, sad, and confused all at once. He took the poster down from the pole, and walked the rest of the way home.

He didn't talk to Mike as he entered the flat. He dumped the bags down in the kitchen and went straight to his room, pulling out his laptop. He takes the poster out of his pocket and finding the website address he saw. Immediately was he blown away by the amount of stuff people had been doing to support his best friend. Several posts had pictures of posters and flyers, and graffiti all over the place. And not just from London. There was pictures from the U.S, Egypt, Poland, Denmark, Switzerland, Canada, everywhere.

And for a moment he can't breathe. He's so touched, by all the support that is being given. He reads posts from old clients. Henry Knight's name pops out at him, and he takes a moment to read the post,

"It saddens me to know that people think Mr. Holmes was a fraud. Because he wasn't. He was the most brilliant man that I have ever met. He knew from when I was a client before I'd even stepped in the door. He knew that I had gotten on the first train from Devon and had a disappointing breakfast. He knew I smoked. He knew I hadn't smoked that day. He knew that the girl I'd met on the train fancied me, and that I'd lost interest. He knew all of this about me, and I had never met this man before in my life. Does that sound like the work of a fraud to you? He solved the case I had brought him, and did my father justice. And I thank him for that. You can read what happened on Dr. John Watson's blog, which brings me onto what I want to say next. John, if you're reading this, I want you to know I still believe, we still believe, in Mr. Holmes. We haven't given up. You changed my life, the both of you. And I thank you. Sherlock Holmes was no fraud. He was a brilliant man. And I owe him my life. - Henry Knight BELIEVES IN SHERLOCK HOLMES."

John found himself crying as he read this, and many posts like it. They all believed, even after all the press had said about him... John logged into his account, and made a post to the page. He explained who he was, and what had really happened in those few months before Sherlock's death. He told them all how touched he was about all the things they've done for Sherlock, and that he'll help in any way he could. He posted this, and went to bed. He'd been reading those posts for hours, it was well past midnight before he went to sleep.

The nightmares came back again that night.

Every night since Sherlock fell from Barts, John's had nightmares. And they're always the same. He sees Sherlock fall from the roof top, he sees Moriarty's face EVERYWHERE. He'd barley slept for months. He'd wake up every morning, crying. But this morning it was different.

He wasn't going to wallow in self pity.

He believes in Sherlock Holmes. He needs to help.

He got out of bed at 4am on a Sunday morning nearing the middle of December, freezing cold, and checked his laptop.

His post made 5000 notes in 4 hours.

Barely able to talk, he scrolls through and looks at some of the comments.

"We believe you, Dr. Watson. What a story!"

"Makes me believe in Sherlock even more, thank you John."

"Please do help the movement, Dr. Watson, we could use your help."

Pulling on a hoodie and some jeans, John headed out onto the streets of London, and didn't return until late that evening.

Within the next four months, Dr. Watson is arrested three times for vandalism and violence (Namely, anyone whom he hears bad mouthing Sherlock gets a punch in the face). 200 hours of community service later, John's back on the streets. Painting the town yellow in graffiti, quite literally.

The movement has grown to a phenomenal scale. Pretty much everyone in the country knows about the movement now. It's rare to find someone in London who doesn't know what's going on, and all the ones who do have some sort of opinion.

One evening, John's flicking through the channels when a news headline pops out at him,

"This is the movement of the century."

The newswoman goes on to explain about the movement, and what it's trying to achieve.

"...The trackable tag on twitter (#BelieveInSherlock) is one of the most trending topics ever. It's hard to find anyone anywhere without an opinion of the stories. Personally? I believe. Back to you in the studio Bob."

John smiles to himself as he watches the report. After a moment, he realised it was being broadcasted on BBC Worldwide. Bigger audience. More people for the movement. he thinks. He turns off the TV and goes back to his laptop. He basically lives on the Internet now, the movement is most popular there. It's the best source of information on the topic. He scrolls through the tweets, smiling as people continuously keep the tag trending. Mike patts John on the back, making him jump.

"You need sleep, mate. I know this means a lot to you, but you can't function on no sleep. You aren't him." The words crumple John's heart. He's been talking about Sherlock for months, why should something this small hurt him so much? The way Mike says it though; it's almost as if he was trying to make a joke, to be sarcastic or funny. He slams the laptop closed and stomps off to his room. He flops onto the bed, and falls asleep immediately. He's more tired than he thought.

The nightmares were worse than ever that night.

He dreams of the day Sherlock jumped off Barts. Except, in his dream, Sherlock doesn't jump: He's pushed. He's pushed off by Moriarty, who laughs maliciously at the sound of Sherlock's yells to John to save him as he plummets to the ground. John sits bolt upright screaming Sherlock's name. It takes him a moment to realise it was just a dream. He lies back down and checks the time: 5:42am. As good a time as any to get up. John rolls slowly out of bed and within minutes is out the door with his spray can. Ready for a new day.

He pushes the dream to the back of his mind as he walks along the street, looking for places that he could graffiti. He bumps into someone as he's moving along. A woman, about his age, maybe a little younger, drops her flyers from the collision. John immediately turns around and starts apologising profusely. He bends down and helps the woman pick up the flyers. Simultaneously, John notices the caption on the paper: Believe in Sherlock, while the woman recognises him.

"You're him. You're John Watson!" She says, practically squealing. They stand together and she shakes her head in embarrassment. "I'm sorry, I just. I'm Mary Morstan. Mr Holmes helped me a few years ago with a case- a problem I had. He really helped me out." John takes Mary's hand and shakes it. She's beautiful. Breathtakingly so. John smiles and looks down at his hands. "Yeah. He was good at that..." After an awkward moment, John looks up at Mary and smiles a little, "Do you- I mean, sorry. It's been a while. Um, do you want to have coffee? With me?" Mary laughs at John's awkward adorableness. She nods, smiling. "Yeah. I'd like that," she says, and walks off to the coffee shop with John.

They get on very well. They stay in that coffee shop for hours; John tells Mary stories of general life in 221b and of cases that he didn't have a chance to write up. Mary tells him of the case Sherlock helped her with. She's a tutor, and after she finishes telling him what happened John certainly sees why Sherlock took the case. They part after three hours, laughing and chatting, with the promise of dinner that evening.

They start dating; regular dinners and movies- The usual. John loves all her little quirks: The way she holds her pen in her mouth when she types; the way she eats her hair when she's thinking; the fact she bites her nails; the fact that she still manages to look beautiful with bed head and no make up. The nightmares stop and, for the first time in a long time, he's happy. Truly happy.

They fall in love. Move in together. And one summer's evening, a little over a year later, Mary and John are wandering through the park near their flat, when John gets down on one knee and asks her to marry him.

She says yes. There's lots of crying and kissing and hugging as they celebrate together with a picnic in the park, watching the sun go down. Mary's favourite time of day is sunset.

The wedding's almost eleven months later; May 14th. Spring wedding. They have the ceremony and the reception outside, and the day is glorious and warm. Sherlock is mentioned in the toast. "The only way this day could be any better, would be if my best friend, Sherlock Holmes, was here. I miss you, Sherlock," says John and raises his glass. He and Mary continued contributing to the movement over those months. It's still talked about, but it calmed down dramatically. Everyone raises their glasses in memory of the great detective, and the festivities begin.

A week after the newly weds return from their honeymoon, a letter comes in the post, addressed to the both of them with a note which reads:

Congratulations, Dr and Mrs Watson, on your marriage. I wish you a long and happy life together, and hope that this will help keep you afloat as the years go on.

The note is unsigned, but the envelope contains a check for £500,000, addressed to them. Mary screams her head off and John can barely breathe. A part of him, a small part of him, believes that the check is from Sherlock. But of course, that is impossible. But in his heart, John feels that he's allowed to hope. That he's allowed to cling onto this little idea that his best friend is still alive, and looking after him still.

3.

Yellow by EW

John stood outside the coffee shop, staring at the yellow graffiti on the side of the building across the street. Leaning heavily on his cane, he took a breath and watched the wall.

People streamed around him like a rock in the sea, glancing at him and then looking away again, continuing with their lives as soon as they were past him. The other sidewalk was just as busy, pedestrians blocking his view of the entire sentence but for an occasional break in the crowd, a dash of yellow, an "o" or an "s".

The blond haired man stood there for a good five minutes before moving on, clutching a brown paper bag with a pastry inside and his coffee in one hand, his cane in the other.

His limp was a little less pronounced, his smile turned up a little more, and he hummed while he read the day's paper.
I BELIEVE IN SHERLOCK HOLMES.

4.
Obituary. By Hannah Rogers

Things were difficult after Sherlock had gone. Of course they were. Losing someone is never easy: it's made all the harder when they had died under a spotlight.

The whole thing was an unholy media circus: when they ran out of people to interview or exploit, they made their own developments. It all began when a leading newspaper printed a full page on Richard Brooks in their Sunday edition (which was far from unusual), then point blank refused to print an obituary for the detective who had plummeted from a roof because of him. Threads were spun about John's outrage, about Mrs Hudson's heartbreak: the truth was that neither of them cared. What difference would some ink on some paper make; Sherlock was gone.

Mrs Hudson was jostled in the street; John clung to his surgery job by his fingernails. The door of Baker Street had begun to tinge yellow from the eggs and paint bombs hurled at it. John stopped buying the paper: he couldn't stand the idea of paying the people who pushed Sherlock off a building. But today a paper was crammed through the letter box: creased like a cheap suit and dog-eared. John picked up the note on it as it he tried to remove it from the door. *"Read me- WW"*

He had no intention of doing so: but the nights were long and empty without the melodies of the violin and the entrance of clients. John could not think of anything better to fill the hours. The obituaries page was circled with red pen, and John held his breath as willed himself not to read yet. Was this what he wanted? How should he feel, to see the name of his friend among the untimely, the elderly and the sick?

To be blunt, it was not he wanted. But neither was it an obituary of Sherlock Holmes. It was better.

"Remembering Cinderella: glass shoes were not the smartest idea- PM"

"In the memory of Superman: he really didn't like green rocks- HR"

"For pigs everywhere: we're sorry bacon tastes so good- CD"

John smiled: he was still not ready to laugh, but it was enough. A small step on a long road. The very last obituary, circled several more times in red, was longer than the others, and clearly cost a great deal to print, judging by the thick paragraph of text which disclaimed it.

"We Believe in Sherlock Holmes: this is a message to Doctor John Watson.

You are not alone in this. We are fighting for the truth to be heard, that Moriarty was real and Richard Brooks was a lie.

If we must mourn fictional characters, we believe we should mourn them all.

We are very sincerely yours, Dr Watson.

-Watson's Warriors."

Pictures in order:

1-6. By bskizzle.tumblr.com

7 & 8. By Bianca Bâzoiu

9. "I Believe in Sherlock" by velvetcar09.tumblr.com

10. "I Believe in Sherlock Holmes" by jamiescreations.tumblr.com

11. By itsamagictrick.tumblr.com

12. "John" by Jule (ashqtara.tumblr.com)

13. By carcrashheartsxox.deviantart.com &
http://imaginative.storenvy.com/

14. "Molly" by Jule (ashqtara.tumblr.com)

15 & 16. By moonblossom.tumblr.com

17. "Moriarty" by Jule (ashqtara.tumblr.com)

18. "Save Undershaw" by Flavia F

19. "Sherlock" by Jule (ashqtara.tumblr.com)

I BELIEVE IN SHERLOCK HOLMES

LET'S HAVE DINNER IA

TRUST
SHERLOCK

TRUST IN JOHN WATSON

RICHARD BROOK
IS INNOCENT

SHERLOCK
LIVES

MORIARTY WAS REAL
I BELIEVE IN
SHERLOCK HOLMES

MORIARTY WAS REAL
I BELIEVE IN
SHERLOCK HOLMES

I BELIEVE IN SHERLOC

I
Sherlock
in
believe
Holmes
in
Sherlock
Holmes
believe
Holmes
Sherlock
believe

I BELIEVE IN
SHERLOCK HOLMES

FIGTHING
JOHN
WATSON'S
WAR

BELIeVE

SHE
KNOWS
THE
TRUTH
Do you?

I AM FIGHTING
JOHN
WATSON'S
WAR

I BELIEVE IN
SHERLOCK
HOLMES

DON'T BELIEVE THE LIES

KEEP
CALM
AND
SAVE
UNDERSHAW

I BELIEVE IN
SHERLOCK

The Game is Afoot

1.

Placebo by floppybelly.tumblr.com

Sherlock appreciated the effort that John had put into this. Really, he did. For a mind of one of the ordinary population, this was incredible work. Sherlock was sure that John thought he had missed no detail, thought of every possibility. But creating a mystery for Sherlock to solve during their dry spell, as carefully crafted as it may have been, simply didn't produce the same effect upon solving when Sherlock could TELL by the little traces left behind by his best friend that it was only a placebo.

The one person Sherlock knew best in the world, did he really think he wouldn't notice?

Even still, Sherlock would have to think of some way to thank John for his effort.

2.

Function by floppybelly.tumblr.com

Sherlock tried to tell John that it seemed his right arm had ceased its function, but all that came out was a strained moan of pain.

"Hold still," John commanded the stubborn detective, "I think your arm is broken. I'm going to try splinting it until the ambulance gets here."

Sherlock was reminded how lucky he was to have a doctor as a best friend. The last thing he observed before blacking out from pain was John ripping his t-shirt into strips to wrap around Sherlock's occupational injury.

3.

Maze by floppybelly.tumblr.com

Sherlock paused for a split second to reference his mental map outlining their route through the maze of London's back alleys and rooftops. It only took a moment to reference the landmarks surrounding them and make a quick and decisive turn down the dark alley next to the Italian restaurant. John trailed behind him, just barely keeping pace with Sherlock's wildly-flailing coattails as he tried to keep track of all the twists and turns and secret shortcuts they'd already taken that night, in hot pursuit of the sniper responsible for their client's recent widowing. Sherlock was certain he knew their quarry's eventual destination, as certainly as he knew every possible way to reach it faster.

John gave up on learning Sherlock's map, and simply focused on keeping up without a fatal misstep.

4.

Balloon by floppybelly.tumblr.com

Sherlock paused to let John catch his breath, the early morning mist dissipating as the two hiked through the forest, boots crunching on the dead leaves and pine needles. They were nearly at their destination, a clearing in the forest filled with a particular flower which made the location famous for its power to attract the rare butterfly; the selfsame one whose scales found on the dead Entomologist had pointed them here.

"Oh Sherlock," John gasped as the stepped into the clearing and found themselves surrounded by colors and the silent fluttering of wings, "It's beautiful! Brilliant!"

Sherlock smiled absentmindedly at John's delight, his attention focused elsewhere. A dull blue scrap of canvas hanging from a branch twenty feet outside the clearing. "Looks like our victim was here after all," Sherlock murmured, "He must have crash-landed his survey balloon."

5.

Brick by floppybelly.tumblr.com

Sherlock reeled as his strength wavered and his legs went out from under him, vision fading in and out a bit. His stomach cramped painfully as he fell to the cobblestones below, the quarry he had been chasing through the streets of London finally able to escape his pursuit. John put their target out of his mind, immediately rushing to Sherlock's side as he gripped a pale wrist between his fingers, quickly reassuring himself that the pulse, while weaker than it ought to have been after running like that, was still there.

John checked Sherlock's other vital signs, coming to the quick diagnoses that his friend had finally exhausted himself, and had collapsed in a fall induced by fatigue and starvation. They'd been on the case for four days now, and John had been keeping a close eye on Sherlock, who had refused to ingest anything solid for fear of it bringing him off of his top game. John had prepared himself for this eventuality, pulling an energy bar out of his pocket after having dragged Sherlock to the side of the alley and propped him up against the brick wall.

The very picture of a caretaker or mother hen, John broke off small pieces of the carb-and-protien-packed brick of food and pressed them gently to Sherlock's lips. "You'll eat this and you'll like it," he insisted, ensuring that Sherlock accepted the food and got a bit of rest. After a few minute's pause, John hauled Sherlock up onto his feet and into Angelo's restaurant, which was only about a block away. Damn their case, he was NOT going to let his flatmate go another minute without a hearty meal. Pasta was as good a choice as any.

6.

Zero at the Bone by S.Strucci

They descended, step by step, Lestrade at front. John felt the hairs on his neck stand up as they approached the bottom. Sherlock took in and analyzed the smell that greeted them- musky, mildewy, and grotesquely rotten around the edges.

The television next to the foot of the stairs was still on. A relic, decades old, with white-blue-black static sparking on its screen and the sound emanating from it a harsh buzz interspersed with eerie humanesque noises. The small and singular basement window was blocked by long-dead potted plants of various sizes and jars of things that had once been alive but now slept suspended in preservatives. The window and television served as the only light sources, the latter giving its surroundings a shifting, unstable glow and the former filtering midday sun through strange liquids and casting the shadows of small corpses about. A black velvet painting of a naked woman hung on the back wall. The room had the feel of a kitschy mausoleum, like that of the bloated corpse of a fifties housewife wearing rotting horn rimmed glasses and gaudy makeup.

John stood in the middle of the room and glanced around.

"Bit creepy, isn't it?"

Sherlock half-chuckled and Lestrade muttered a, "Yeah".

On the wall behind the television hung dust-encrusted records surrounding a small, framed, and grimy Elvis Presley photograph. Towards the center of the room and facing the TV was an old reclining chair with a corpse in it. Female, late thirties. She'd been dead for a couple of days and the pleasant and warm summer weather hadn't done her any favors. The death itself probably wasn't quick and it certainly wasn't painless. She'd been mauled. Partially dismembered. Possibly partially eaten.

Sherlock crouched and used a gloved hand to gently examine her fingernails.

John studied the low bookshelf in the corner. It was full of books on human and animal anatomy, various sciences, and the occult, with several volumes not in English and a couple in languages he didn't recognize. The bookshelf had a tacky multicolored lamp adorning it. John attempted to click it on. Nothing happened. He leaned a little closer and realized that while it was plugged in, it had no bulb.

"There's another one in the bathroom," said Lestrade, gesturing to a half-open door at the back of the room. "Haven't ID'd them yet due to shady leasing practices and missing purse and wallet but we'll have 'em soon enough through dental records."

John gently pushed the door open further and stepped in while Sherlock continued his examination. Bright, green-blue tile covered the floor and combination shower/bathtub wall and juxtaposed with the faded mustard yellow wallpaper and inky grime between the tiles. There was no shower curtain.

A yellowed and exposed bulb in a naked fixture protruded from the ceiling. Watson flicked the switch on. Luckily, this one actually worked. There was another body, as Lestrade had mentioned. It laid half on the floor, half draped over the side of the bathtub, with its face and middle ripped up. Male, around the same age, though it was difficult to tell from the state of his remains. The cabinet under the sink appeared to have been raided. Partially dried blood pooled near the drain and flecked a few places on the tile where it had sprayed. There was a human heart in the toilet.

Sherlock stepped in and carefully assessed the bathroom. Lestrade followed, though he didn't leave the doorway. Sherlock swung open the mirror, behind which stood a few rows of empty pill bottles. After examining them, he glanced down at the toilet.

"Our killer has a sense of humor, at least."

Lestrade groaned.

Sherlock ducked down and examined the sink cabinet. John, not sure of what to do with himself, leaned over the edge of the bathtub to get a closer look at the corpse.

Still bent down and studying but content to begin an assessment, Sherlock spoke.

"The killings appear to have been done by some sort of beast. There was a person accompanying it, though." He tapped the top of the sink from the inside. "Something was hidden right here.

There are adhesive marks left from duct tape. No blood on the cleaning supplies thrown about, so the killer waited until the two were dead before searching."
Lestrade stepped in a little further. "Sherlock-"
"She physically put up a fight- there's caked flesh and blood under her fingernails, and I made out some defensive wounds despite the state of her body- but he didn't. Three scenarios right off the bat from that. It's possible he was attacked first, though it's obviously fairly unlikely that killer and companion could have just waltzed right by her unnoticed. If they somehow managed that, her proximity means that she would have at least come in to investigate the sound of flesh being torn up."
"Sherlock! We-"
"It's possible she was attacked first, but he certainly would have heard it. Maybe he was deaf and couldn't hear her or had some sort of other impairment or disability, on his own or due to the killer, but that doesn't seem likely for either of them. From the positions and state of the corpses, the most likely and most sinister scenario is that one of them knew that the other would be be attacked and let it-"
"Sherlock!"
Sherlock finished up his study of the cabinet's wooden paneling then looked up at Lestrade. "Hmm?"
"We know all that. Give us some credit."
"If you knew that," said John, "then why-"
"Why waste our time?" finished Sherlock.
"We mostly wanted your help on determining cause of death. None of us have been able to figure out which animal, er, which 'beast' did it. It's too early for any lab analysis, obviously, and we expect to know eventually, but we were stumped and wanted a hunch and a head start."
Sherlock stared at a patch of mold on the corner of the bathtub for a few seconds then abruptly stood up and turned to face Lestrade.
"No idea."
"Surely, you-"

"I mentioned that they appear to have been done by a beast. The ferocity and brute strength indicates an animal, obviously, but the claw and bite marks don't match anything I've previously encountered. The bite marks specifically are rather large and indicate the teeth of a carnivore but jaw shape itself is fairly humanoid. I'd suggest some kind of fake or staged attack, but, again, the sheer strength and violence of the inflicted wounds suggests otherwise."

Lestrade crossed his arms. "You've got nothing, then?"

"Samples from the woman's fingernails and elsewhere ought to be at least somewhat conclusive. I'd appreciate photographs of the wounds for further analysis and comparison later along with victim identities so I can investigate them and their relation to the eccentric décor. I'll also do some research of my own on the assortment of books they've got piled up. If I think of anything else, I'll keep in touch."

Lestrade glanced at John. John shrugged.

"Thanks for coming down, I, uh, guess. You two know the way out. Five minutes is up anyway."

Sherlock exited the bathroom, paused for a moment in front of the bookcase to take a couple of photos with his phone, and ascended the stairs. John followed.

Once they were in a cab and out of earshot, John turned to Sherlock, eyebrows raised.

"'Nothing'?"

"No fooling you, is there?" said Sherlock, putting away his phone in a shirt pocket after having spent a few minutes studying the photographs he'd taken (some of the books and some he'd snuck of the corpses beforehand).

"Let's have it, then!" said John after a decidedly smug pause of several seconds on Sherlock's part.

"Did you recognize the woman in the chair?"

"Maybe? Er, she looked familiar, but I wasn't sure."

"If her glasses and bone structure hadn't been mostly intact the job would've been much more difficult. Would have been even easier if she were wearing a white lab coat, though."

"You don't mean-"
"Yes, John. Baskerville."
"God. I was hoping we were rid of that place."
"Nope!" said Sherlock, almost smiling. "I'd venture to say that whatever was stolen out from under the sink might be related to her place of employment."
"And if it is you lied so that you could find out with minimal interference from Lestrade and any other members of the English government, correct?"
"Naturally."

7.

The Adventure of the Poisoned Affair By Luke Benjamen Kuhns

An Excerpt from the Personal Diaries of Doctor John H. Watson: The Adventure of the Poisoned Affair.

I have been asked to briefly recap the Adventure of the Poisoned Affair not for the sake of telling a good story but in the hopes that the names involved in this affair can be cleared. Though the entire story is written in my notes and I do wish to publish it in full length however the shortness of time has propelled me to miss out on some of the intriguing elements of this case and skip to the chase. I must be brief; as Holmes would say, time is of the essence.

Doctor John H. Watson

Feb '89

PART 1:

"How do you know you are who you think you are?" Asked Sherlock Holmes. I was shocked at the phrase that uttered from his mouth. Very little time did he devote to philosophical or theological questions.
"Good, God Holmes, where did that come from?" I asked
"It was just a thought. Have you ever wondered, Watson, about the people we have met? The good the bad; some times I think what these people might not have been, who they were had they not been corrupted by the infectious disease of crime."
"I say Holmes, I can't but agree. However, I am stunned at this sudden change to philosophical questions." I said,
"Is it philosophical to try and understand the human condition and what a person would have been in another frame?
To us we see people either effected, hurt, or killed by crime or people who are either effecting, hurting or killing for crime. For us we see people through these lenses. But nevertheless these

people are more than that. They are son's or daughters, Mothers, Fathers, Friends, even colleagues.
And that is what begs the question: how do you know you are who you think you are, as we are all different people to different people."

It took me some time to respond to my friend's thought. I had no idea what seed was planted into his mechanical brain to produce a thought such as this, but if one man could turn a philosophical thought into a clear deduction of the human condition it was most certainly Sherlock.
"Well Holmes," I finally said, "I suppose you are right. Indeed, to change ones perspective will inevitably help one gain further understanding of the ever-changing human condition."
"And so it should." He finished and reached for his pipe as he raised from his seat and packed it full.
"Identity Watson," Holmes said as he lit his pipe and glared out the window, "its becoming an ever growing concern, and I would go as far as to say that in the near future every-ones struggle for identity will inevitably lead to an identity-confused society."
"Holmes, any deduction you make - whether it be on the simplest of things of the grandest - I would wholeheartedly accept your judgement." I replied.
"And so it would seem we have a visitor," said Holmes changing the topic from one we would never bring up again bar once.

After our conversation a young woman was brought into our study. She was the wife of Jackson Hardy, a famous world traveler and explorer. Mrs Hardy informed us that the previous day her husband was found dead in his study with a suicide note on his desk and a bottle of poison on the floor. Mrs Hardy swore on her life that Jackson was not the type to commit such an horrendous act. Inspector Gregson, who was on the scene, had written the case off as a simple suicide Mrs Hardy told us. Holmes saw something in this woman, in her voice, and he agreed to

investigate. We journeyed out to Mrs Hardy's Wembley Manor where Holmes began his investigation.
The Hardy house was full of plants both harmless and harmful and surrounded by weapons from all over the world. Mrs Hardy gave Holmes and myself access to look through the study where Jackson's body was found for clues, as well as other areas of the house. We noticed a strange relationship between Mrs Hardy and a man named Thomas Strong who was Jackson's friend and partner on many of his adventures. After a few days piecing a the puzzle together and doing an autopsy on the body of Mr Jackson, Hardy Holmes and I found ourselves back at the Wembley Manor for one last time. Holmes had discovered that the poison found in the bottle was not the poison that killed Jackson Hardy.

I walked up the spiral stair and entered the study. It looked untouched. Holmes had been looking through the desks putting out papers and reading anything that caught him.
"Ah Watson, anything for me?"
"I found a letter"
"Let us have it then."
He took it and read it through, "This is very interesting Watson. Here, read this now." and Holmes handed me the large leather book. I started reading where Holmes pointed, and it said:

"For some time now Tim has been fighting feelings for my wife. This has caused me much pain as I am torn between my two best friends."
Another entry read:
"We are in India, I want to enjoy myself but I can't, he has gone to far. I feel that I may kill him now. I found a letter he gave to Lilly. He was begging her for her hand. I have found it best to part ways with Tim. Lilly and I are traveling without him until we get to China where we will talk."
"We got to China. Tim was in trouble. Couldn't leave him, feared for his life. Managed to free him by bribery and villainy. I find it

hard to part with him, as he is my friend, my brother. He begged me for forgiveness and asked to join us once again."

"My God, Holmes. Timothy Strong was in love with Mrs Hardy?" said I,
"Yes. And rather ardently I would say." remarked Holmes who was sitting on the couch were Mr Hardy was found dead just days ago. Something tweaked in Holmes mind then. The wheels were spinning faster than ever. He burst from his seat and walked over to the large clock on the mantel.
He pressed his fingers around the circular face. Where the arms of the clock meet in the middle Holmes noticed a hole. A very small hole indeed. To me it looked as if a screw had fallen out but to Holmes it was something else.
After a few clicks and found that the clock was far more than that. The entire front of it opened up and came off and inside built into the workings of the clock was an automatic dart gun.

Holmes raced over the couch where he threw the pillows off and lo sitting there was a dart. Holmes picked it up and smelt it and ran his finger a long it. He tasted the tip of his finger and spat on the ground.
"This Watson, is the poison that killed Mr Hardy."

"Watson, the game is afoot!" said Sherlock, "and now its time to set the bait!" We were interrupted by foots coming up the stairs.
"Mrs Hardy?" Sherlock asked
"Yes, Mr Holmes." she said in a low tone voice.
"We have obtained a considerable amount of evidence here,"
"Mr Holmes, Doctor Watson. I'm sorry. I think I've sent you on a wild goose chase. I know what Tim said in his talk with you, and if it was one of the many people they angered on their trips, the odd of finding them are slim. And after a lot of thought I think it's best for you two to leave...in fact tomorrow morning I will be gone. I'm going back to Cape Town with Timothy."
"Mrs Hardy, I do not recommend an action like that." said I,

"Doctor Watson, you have been most kind, both of you have. But I fear this is the right action to take." said Mrs Hardy.
"Mrs Hardy I have to agree with Doctor Watson, you leaving will make things worse for you."
"Nevertheless, this is my road. Thank you both for you assistance. But I asked you to look into an impossible problem"
Holmes and I did not speak for a few moments while we compiled ourselves and walked down the stairs.
"Goodbye Mr Holmes and Doctor Watson,"
"Goodbye Ma'am."

"We are running out of time Watson," said Sherlock as we walked towards the cart, "We must take action tonight. But it must be quick and it must be secretive!"
We rushed to the nearest telegraph station and sent a message to Gregson asking him to meet us Wembley. Luckily we were responded too within a few minuets, and we waited for Gregson.
"Holmes, what is the plan?" I asked,
"The plan, to arrest Mrs Hardy for the murder of Mr Hardy."

PART 2:

"You must be joking!" I cried, "She came to us! Why would she do that,"
"Guilt. Watson. She wanted to be discovered."
"How did you come to this conclusion?!"
"Patient Watson. Here is Gregson."
Sure enough Gregson was pulling up to us. He stepped out of the police cab and shook our hands,
"Hello sirs, what do you have for me?"
"Gregson. I need you to arrest Mrs Hardy." said Holmes
"Seriously?" asked Gregson
"Yes." said Holmes.

We joined Gregson in the cab and made our way towards the Hardy estate. We approached the door and Holmes knocked. Mrs Hardy answered and her face was shocked to see us.
"Holmes, I told you this was over, please leave me now."
"Mrs Hardy, I'm afraid were are here for you. You are under the arrest for the murder of Mr Hardy." said Gregson
"Holmes, you can't be serious!" she cried, "Doctor Watson?"

Gregson took Mrs Hardy by the hands and cuffed her. It pained me to see her being treated like this. He walked her to the cab and put her inside. I was distracted by yelling and saw Mr Strong running across the lawn towards us!
"Hold it there you fool!" he cried charging up on us, "What are you doing?"
"We are arresting her for the murderer of Mr Hardy." said Holmes
"Holmes, you have lost your mind. She did not do it!"
"Mr Strong, you will be able to see her when she is properly contained." said Gregson,
"Lilly! I will follow you there!"
"Gregson, will you stay behind with me, and Watson, please assist Mrs Hardy to the jail." said Holmes, "Oh, and Watson, here." said Holmes as he handed me a piece of paper, "do not read it until you are there."
"I won't, don't worry Holmes."

I road with all the way to the jail with a not in my stomach. I could see Mr Strong's cart rinding up behind us. In my hand was Holmes's note. I looked at it and on the back it said,
"Read me now"
So I opened the letter and it said,

"Watson, I'm sorry to put you through all this. Also apologies to Mrs Hardy. All will be clear and her name will not be scared. Keep Mrs Hardy company and I will meet you both there tonight.
SH"

I felt a great relief take me. I had no idea how Holmes had come to a conclusion of Mrs Hardy, but to find out he was playing a game, made me feel better. I turned and saw Mrs Hardy crying.
"Lilly," I said and she turned to look at me.
"Do not worry. All will be clear, trust Holmes."
"I don't see how I can when he's put me here,"
"Not all is what it seems dear Lilly."

We arrived at the station and Lilly was taken to a cell. I told her to be calm but that was easier to say than to do. Once she was in her cell I walked outside and found Mr Strong. He grabbed me and shoved me against the wall,
"Whatever the hell your friend Sherlock has done, he will pay the price for it!"
"I suggest you take your hands off me unless you want to find yourself in a cell next to Lilly!" I demanded.
He let me go and stormed into the station demanding to see Lilly.
Feeling rather parched and assuming Mrs Hardy was too, I went out and got some food for us. When I returned to the station Mr Strong had been gone for a while and Lilly was sitting in the cell.
"Guard!" I called and moments later one came running up,
"Yes Doctor,"
"Let her out," I said
"Yes, sir," said the guard unlocking the cell.
"I, I don't understand." she stammered
"Neither do I, yet. but you must be hungry so let's eat and wait here for Holmes." said I.

Finally about 4 hours later there was a commotion outside. Several guards were carrying in a body. I got up to see what was going on when I saw Sherlock.
"Holmes!" I yelled
"Ah, Watson, there you are. and Mrs Hardy? Oh good, good to see you both." Holmes walked over to Mrs Hardy and embraced her,
"I am terribly sorry for arresting you. But know that it was all a trap to catch the real killer of your husband."

"And who is that!" she demanded
"Mrs Hardy, I am sorry to tell you this, but your husbands real killer, was Mr Strong.

Her face froze, she didn't know what to think. Her knees started to shake and she fell back, but we caught her and sat her in a chair. When the colour arrived in her face she took a sip of water which Holmes had got for her.
"Holmes, you really must explain." she said

"I will. You see, the weapon that killed your husband was a trap set by someone who knew his habits. It was not an overdose like Gregson and Lestrade believed at first, no indeed. Rather inside the large clock on the mantel was that a automatic dart gun. And when your Husband went into his study that day at 2:45 someone knew what he would do. They knew that he liked to sit and read for awhile, they also knew that your husband didn't hold books or maps close to his face making his face and neck a prime target, and set the clock to fire a dart at the exact time he would be sitting and reading. The dart struck the left of his neck, he pulled it out and it fell into the couch where he died. And someone put a bottle of poison and a suicide note on the table to cover their own tracks.
Now how did I know it was Strong? His obsession with you. From the very first meeting he did not like having other people around you. When we returned after examining your husbands body, he was there and we heard you having an argument about going away. Watson heard him argue with you again after we spoke with him about there being nothing in your way, and not long after that conversation you came up and told us that you were leaving and to drop the case. Now why would you do that? I knew you were not the killer, but I knew the killer had to be close. So I set the trap. I wanted to see Mr Strong's reaction to your being arrested.
While he followed you to the station I took the large clock with the help of Gregson and we put it in his house, in the living space. And there I waited for Strong to return. He came back sooner than I thought he would and when he did he saw the clock. Frantically he

looked around the room to see if anything was out of place. Perhaps his own nightmare of something from his past catching up to him was coming true. When he approached the clock, I set the final trap. I rigged the clock fire a dart when I pressed a trigger. The dart sunk into Strong neck and immediately he felt the effects.
No, no, he won't die. I simply created a compound from the plant inside your house Mrs Hardy that would paralyze his muscles and make him think he was dying.
While he laid on the ground I stepped out of the shadows and he pleaded for help. While he lay there going numb I told him his game was up. And that we knew he was the murderer. He didn't want money, he didn't want anything except the one thing he never had and always envied. You Mrs Hardy.
Mr Strong admitted that it was true. When he heard of your plan to leave England and not take him with you he set up a trap to kill his friend and take his wife, the woman he loved but only from a distance.
Indeed your husband was not depressed nor did he commit suicide. However the only true thing was the note, however those words belong to another man, Mr Strong."

Mrs Hardy eyes were dripping with tears, and I had put my arm around her for comfort. She looked at Holmes speechless before she turned and embracing me. I looked at Holmes and Gregson who was standing behind now and Holmes walked up and put his hand on Mrs Hardy's head, leaned in near her ear and said,
"I'm terribly sorry for you loss my dear."
When we arrived at Baker Street and found our way into the study, Sherlock Holmes turned to me and said, "They were not just a dead man, a widow, and a jealous friend. No. They were friends and brothers, and lovers. The human condition, I think, will never be fixed, but maybe we can help it."

The End.

8.

Lantern by floppybelly.tumblr.com

Watson ran his hand along the cave wall, shuddering as it quickly became coated in a damp slime. He could hardly see where his feet were going, or even what he was stepping on, as the light from the lantern which Holmes carried was so dim and so much further ahead in the underground passage. "Holmes!" he hissed, surprised by how loudly his voiceless call echoed in the tunnel, "Wait the bloody hell up! Your target is dead, remember? He won't be going anywhere any time soon!"

Holmes paused and lit a cigarette from the stout, oil-fed flame, and smoked it impatiently while Watson struggled to keep up. "If the rats destroy any evidence before we get to it, I'm blaming you," he muttered, puffing just once or twice before stubbing the end out on the damp wall. Wouldn't do to flood the cavern with smoke, after all, what with visual conditions as compromised as they already were

He offered an arm as Watson finally reached him, which the shorter man gladly took, ensuring a safe journey through these wretched caves as they followed their map of clues.

9.
Blanket by Leslie Mahoney

It had been days since Sherlock had slept, but John didn't really worry. Of course he worried a little bit–with the protectiveness he felt for Sherlock and his doctor's instinct how could he not? But he knew that eventually Sherlock's body would shut down, (despite Sherlock's protests), and force him to rest. And so when John came home that night after a slow day at the clinic, the sight of Sherlock slumped in his usual armchair did not surprise him in the least, and it brought a smile to the tired doctor's weary face and a certain contentedness to his heart. He imagined it was how a parent must feel after watching their child struggle for days on end and then at long last find peace.

He saw Sherlock's bare feet and noticed that he wasn't wearing his coat and scarf either. So he went to his room, grabbed the blanket off the bed, and came back into the study. He knew he didn't have to worry about waking Sherlock up, so he took as much force as necessary to properly wrap the blanket around the detective.
He took a step back, smiled, and then walked into the kitchen to fix himself a snack.

When Sherlock awoke at noon the next day, John had already gone to work. At first the blanket had confused him, but then he recognized it as the one from John's room. He looked at the door, knowing that it would be the one that John would enter through in a few hours, and smiled. As though he were actually there.

10.
An Excerpt from the Personal Accounts of John H. Watson
Authored by Sylvia Yi

It wasn't long before Sherlock and I found ourselves standing outside the dingy pub where the suspect had dashed in just a moment before. DI Lestrade and a few of his men were inside as we had tipped them off earlier, so we weren't as anxious at the cumbersome task of preventing him from escaping our clutches. I leaned against the cold brick wall to my left to catch my breath while Sherlock, the less athletic of us both, followed suit. Unlike Holmes who had spent the majority of his days researching at St. Bart's laboratory, I have had a long enough experience in the British Army and games of rugby to build the strength necessary to better endure such lengthy endeavours, although I must inform you that Mr. Holmes, however, is most capable in his own ways. He is an excellent swordsman and boxer and I fear that my own physical adeptness has much declined since my involvement in Afghanistan.

I hadn't realized how much time had elapsed since my last thought of Afghanistan occurred. I used to dream of the horrors of the battlefield, awaking at odd hours of the night until the unforgiving stream of light from the rising sun of dawn mocked my futile attempt to ease my tired mind and reminded me that another sleepless night had expired. It was most difficult to adjust to civilian life. Every time I shut my eyes, I was back on the battlefield: my shoulder was bleeding; I was aware of the horrid pain of my bone shattering and subclavian artery barely being grazed by a Jezail bullet mere moments before a figure grabbed my body and hoisted me up onto a packhorse, Murray, my orderly, if I'm not mistaken was that very man with the heart of courage and to whom I owe my life.

Upon falling ill with an intense fever, it was seen fit by the medical board to send me promptly back to England. In hopes of seeking liberation from the achingly dreadful relations of those I had left behind when I left to join the army, I arrived in London soon after, but every night I would awake in a cold sweat, a slave to my nightmares. The dreams were relentless. Even in my subconscious thoughts, I could hear the screams. I'd walk down the cobblestone streets where civilians would bustle about; it was far too much for my health and sanity. I felt the suffocation of people closing in on my everywhere. I remembered the sound of discharging weapons, a whole multitude of bullets being shot from every direction imaginable. The smell of death and the feeling of fear lingered at the back of my mind not only in my dreams but in every waking moment. I'd lie there trapped in a hellish state, too exhausted to stay up, but much too shaken to go back to sleep. That is, until I met one Mr. Sherlock Holmes.

I looked over at him leaning over his legs, attempting to replenish his direly needed supply of oxygen in the cold, harsh, winter air. Mycroft, Sherlock's older brother, had informed me that I was good for Sherlock as God knows he had always fussed about his younger brother and his 'uniqueness', as he put it, but perhaps he had never noticed that I was in emotional requirement of him as well. All it took was a single act of fate to bring two halves together and change the course of destiny for two men like ourselves. And fate, they name is Stamford (if you don't recall, my former dresser who had introduced us some time ago when I needed a place to live, but preferred a housemate to share the fee with). Now I dreamt of triumph. I dreamt of justice. No longer was I afraid of the chase and thrill. Fear did not deter me. My shoulder no longer hurt and the limp I had sustained in my leg was gone. I do not recall when it had ceased to become a bother, but I no longer rose with the sun and laid awake in discomforting agony. Sometimes I'd lie in silence in my desolate room at our flat at 221B Baker Street, listening to the beautiful melodies Sherlock played on his violin while he was in one of his 'states', thinking, reflecting, attempting to solve a puzzle. He could go on like this for days without eating or moving. He was fascinating. Brilliant. When we met to discuss our potential residential arrangement, he knew everything about me in a single glance while I, on the other hand, knew nothing of him.

Over time, I began to know more of the enigma named 'Sherlock Holmes'. He claimed that he was quite an adept consulting detective, but I learned of his limits, his strange philosophies, and his rather bizarre bohemian lifestyle. But soon, I found myself involved with his strange escapades. I had ultimately become Dr. John H. Watson, partner to the great Sherlock Holmes, assisting in solving crimes baffling to Detective Inspector Lestrade and his men while chronicling our adventures together. The people we meet call him a cold analytic machine and ask me why I tolerate such a man, but surely they do not know who he is or what he's really like underneath his cold disposition. His loyalty to myself is as undeniable just as my loyalty to him is as irrefutable. I caught a glimpse of his heart behind his cold façade once when I received a superficial bullet wound by a man we were attempting to capture. Sherlock's demeanor had noticeably changed. His firm lips were shaking and his cold eyes dimmed out of fear for me as I stood point-blank in front of the face of Death once again. I was touched and humbled that a great man such as himself allowed me at least a moment to bear witness to his vulnerability. Long before that, we had already come to a fluidity in our partnership, but this moment had confirmed me that all the time we spent together as partners had accumulated into a treasured friendship. He unknowingly relies on me perhaps more than I do on him, but that does not change the mere fact that we are equals. Yes, I must admit, I do irritate him, but I prompt him to think clearer. Faster. He teaches me to think outside the normality of what is; after all, in his words, I've learned that when you have eliminated the impossible, whatever remains, however improbable, must be the truth.

Sherlock noticed my short glance at him and he immediately straighted up as his body completed restoring his much needed oxygen and his irregular breathing returned to normal. Suddenly, we jumped as a couple of cracks of gunshots rand in the air behind us. Faintly, we could hear Lestrade and his men yelling orders above the sound of the patrons screaming and running towards the door to escape outside to safety.

"Shall we my dear boy, Watson?" he asked with a slight hint of a smile and a glint in his eye as he reached in his breast pocket for his pistol—it was undeniable, how he loved the thrill of chase.

"Ready when you are, Mr. Holmes," I responded cheekily as I grasped at my own cold

iron. We both pushed off the wall and proceeded to run inside the pub after the man who had evaded us for far too long in my opinion. The game is, undeniably, now afoot.

11.

By captainactiongrammarmom.tumblr.com

The night was chilled and clear. Sherlock lay quite still, and barely noticed as his breath puffed out before him, distracted by something else entirely. He elbowed Watson, who lay next to him sleeping, and woke him.

"Watson," he said, "Look up. Tell me what you see, and what you make of it."

John Watson looked up at the sky above him and saw a vast expanse of stars, unhindered by cloud cover or the lights of London and was glad to have come camping with his friend and flatmate.

"Well, Holmes," he conjectured, "I suppose the vastness of the heavens suggests that there may be life on other planets. That we'd be quite foolish to consider ourselves absolutely alone."

Sherlock turned his head and fixed his companion with a scornful look. "No, Watson. It means that someone has stolen our tent."

He sat and surveyed their surroundings with great attention to detail. "Or, more specifically, they've stolen us. "

Watson sat in a hurry and looked about, gasping in shock, "But how, Holmes?"

"How indeed," he replied, crouching over the ground near where they'd been laying.
"There were five of them, and they came just up this way," he deduced, pointing slightly downhill and to the south, "Two of them carried each of us, at head and foot, without removing us from our sleeping bags, and the fifth followed, most likely directing them. She must have wanted us out of the way for some time."

"She, Holmes?" Watson inquired.

"Yes, 'she', Watson. No man walks with his steps so in line." Holmes continued, "We're looking for a woman, with knowledge of our plans to go out and to where, with four able-bodied men at her disposal, and with business she did not want me getting into occurring in or near London tomorrow morning. "

"Well, what do we do now, Holmes?"

"We go after them." he responded, helping his friend to his feet, "By going home."

They set off in the direction that Sherlock had indicated, following a set of footsteps when John noticed something peculiar. "Sherlock?" he said, pointing to the fifth set of footsteps, supposedly belonging to a woman, "These footsteps are pointing in the same direction that we're walking. Shouldn't we be going in the opposite direction? I saw a set of prints coming from the woods, as well, and they were headed in this direction. Surely the gang of miscreants that abducted us did so from that direction?"

Sherlock stopped and crouched near to the ground again, pointing, "No, Watson, look closer." he said, "Really look. These footsteps here are a few inches deeper than the ones headed off into the forest. They must have been carrying something then, something heavy. Us. And these here, the woman's— Look at how shallow they are at the heel, barely there. Now look at the toes, they're much deeper."

He looked up at Watson, hoping that he'd caught on by now. After a second's silence, he lost patience and explained it to him, "She was walking backwards, John, obviously. I can guarantee that if we'd have followed their trail into the forest, we'd have ended up miserably lost, and been ambushed as soon as we came upon the way out."

"Incredible." Watson expressed, straightening up and shaking his head, half impressed and half in dismay at the thought of attackers coming at them from behind trees. He followed Sherlock a good way down the slope and sure enough, as the moon sunk in the sky, they came upon what had once been their campsite. The tent had, indeed, been stolen, as had everything else, but there was still a bit of char and rubble left where their campfire had once been. From there, it was fairly easy to find their way back to 221b Baker street.

12.

Sherlock Holmes and the Adventure of the Wrongly Named by Martin Shone

It was his pipe that saved our sanity that day. It was a dull day and I was bored, Holmes was bored and looking out the window I could see London was bored too. The leaves from autumn trees seemed to droop and relax as they floated to earth.

"I say Holmes."
"Hmm?" He turned to me while reaching languidly behind him for his pipe. Even with his long fingers he only managed to squeeze the pipe's stem between his thumb and forefinger before it tipped and fell. "Well Watson! What do you make of that?"
"Mrs Hudson will have something to say, Holmes. Another burn mark in her carpet."
"Look, Watson, don't you see it? Oh I've been a fool."
"Yes, Holmes. Quick pick it up."
"Leave it, Watson and look."
Holmes sprang from his chair and pounced beneath the table to where the pipe's ash lay smouldering.
"Holmes, old man what is it?"
"Don't you see, look at the ash."
"Well, the ash is, Oh I don't know, Holmes."
"Use my methods, Watson. What do you make of it?"

I could see a small mound of cooling ash within an increasing ring of singe. Little swirls of dusty smoke reached my nostrils. The pipe lay upon its side.

"Holmes, I see ash, your pipe and smoke."
"Watson, you make the simple man in the street clever by comparison, open your eyes man."
Quite used to his brusque nature, I remarked, "Holmes, what can't I see?"
He made a dash for the door, "Come Watson! A man's life is at stake."

I stamped on the ash and darted after him.

Seeing how the ash and pipe had fallen, Holmes had deduced in that split second that Mr George Williams-Brown was innocent.

Pictures in order:

1. "A Three Patch Problem" by naturalshocks.tumblr.com
2. By clenniecarps.tumblr.com
3. By coeykuhn.com
4. By enscade.tumblr.com
5. "Hanging Over London" by sherllllock.tumblr.com
6. By jamiescreations.tumblr.com
7. By lilywinterwood.tumblr.com
8. By oly-rrr.tumblr.com
9. By ottoman.tumblr.com

Deduce, John Deduce!
I am Deducing Sherlock!

RACH

When you walk with Sherlock Holmes
you see the battlefield.

221b

Beneath the Hat

1.

By smilethedaysaway.tumblr.com

And so many may wonder about his figure named Sherlock Holmes—This mysterious, magical man who can perceive so much with but the simplest of glances. We may gaze and ponder and look upon him with awe, yet it is a scarce moment when any of us mortals may ogle him with understanding. Beneath a dark and suave outward appearance, hidden behind the layers of cold and calculating deductions lies a man who cannot be categorized. A sociopath? No. He cannot be anything in the likes if merely for the way he cares for his colleague. So this stereotype for a man so quickly dismissed as mad, even autistic at times, is just as false as the idea of a right handed man who committed suicide even when the bullet was on the left side. This man is indescribable. He is iconic. He is a good man—A great man. He is one that shall last though our age, those to come and perhaps Sherlock Holmes will be looked upon as the true savior of London that he truly was, even if it was in the world of literature, parchment and leather binding.

2.

Below by floppybelly.tumblr.com

It wasn't that Sherlock thought it below himself to do such mundane things as buying milk or cleaning the bathroom, (though John wouldn't be surprised to learn that to be the case) it was just another one of those things he chose not to save into his mental hard drive. Manners and excessive hygiene and taking turns, why give up the phone numbers of all his previous clients for the past ten years in exchange for something so menial?

John couldn't say he liked Sherlock's choice of knowledge, but it was something he understood. So when he had to remember every time to stock the fridge full of something other than body parts, he only sighed and hoped it was worth it.

3.

Orbit by floppybelly.tumblr.com

John had been genuinely surprised to learn of Sherlock's ignorance of the Earth's orbit. To be fair, the knowledge would rarely factor in to most human motives. It was just... John wondered what else Sherlock was ignorant about. Would he know what chemicals had flammable properties? Which bones would need immediate treatment when broken? How to start a fire when stranded in the woods?

John tried to stop worrying, assuring himself that whenever another one of Sherlock's gaps in knowledge surfaced, he would be there to fill it in.

4.

Butterfly by floppybelly.tumblr.com

Sherlock peered into his microscope, careful not to breathe too forcefully and blow away the delicate wing-scales. This was his last lead on the entomologist, the honey samples had turned up nothing of interest. If he could just glean a few particulates off of these butterfly scales, he might be able to tell where the body had come from, or what had been in contact with it.

It only occurred to Sherlock halfway in that he might look at the scales themselves; Butterflies tended to be very regional, if he could identify the species and even sub-species, he might be able to track it to its natural area. It was a long shot, but without further evidence, it was the best he had. He wondered how John would feel about a trip to a butterfly mating ground, wherever that might turn out to be.

5.

Addiction by floppybelly.tumblr.com

Sherlock bent over the lab set of his most recent addiction, the tobacco ash having been exhausted in every last type and possibility. The latest case they had just solved had left Sherlock with a lingering interest in Entomology; it had been a thrill to be able to trace a location by the species of butterfly, or the contents of honey, and Sherlock could see the practicality of using insect behavioural patterns as important markers. They would be a useful resource in future cases, should any particulates of that sort be found again.

The obsessive detective, in his spare time between cases, had already worked his way through cataloging the more-than-thousand species of Lepidoptera; he had sorted them by ease of identification and proximity to London. Now he had started on the honey, testing countless samples for their chemical makeups and other marking factors. John didn't mind this one so much, it was less delicate and left the flat smelling of warm honey every time Sherlock booted up the burners. He almost wondered if he was starting to become addicted to the leftover samples, which Sherlock had allowed him to add to his tea.

6.

A Study in Fiction by Rachel Richardson

"Why are you so weird?"

"Yeah, it's just sad that you think you're our friend."

"Exactly! Just leave."

Words of the cruel girls cut her deeply and she curls up in the corner of the room. Sad and alone. Again....It's been like this for years, now. Always confused, always misunderstood...always lonely. Her friends are all fake. Everyone is an enemy here. The girl wants to sink into the ground and die, to never have to face the world of cruel peers she is trapped in.

But then they walk in. The two greatest people in the girl's life. The two gentlemen come for her - so different and yet so similar. They are the ones who she truly trusts. The ones who will never hurt her. The tall, eccentric one did break her heart once before, but those circumstances were different. He was protecting the other man. The quieter one. The man the girl wished to, one day, find a friend just like him to keep to herself.

The pair give her gentle smiles as they pull her from her corner of isolation. They know how to make it all go away. They know how to cheer her up and make her smile. They know everything about her. The two men hold either of her hands as they walk down the narrow road. No one looks at them. No one really notices. Then again, no one ever really does when they're here.

The two men have brought her to their father's house. A man whom the girl adores to no end. Brushing back blond hair from her sad eyes, she grips the hands of her friends tightly and smiles at the new addition to her company of irregulars. The young girl wants nothing more than to pour out her pure admiration and affection to the father of her most trustworthy companions. To say how much she loves and respects him....

"Your books are genius, they are my favourites," she wants to say. "I love them! I love the stories, the adventure, the danger! I wish I could be half as skilled as you."

But she never can tell him. Even if she could, the man would think nothing of the praise. Absolutely nothing at all. But the words are there in her thoughts, and that is good enough.

She looks back to her friends, thanking them with her eyes for bringing her here to see this man at work. She nods at the tall man in the deerstalker, and smiles widely as she salutes the equally as brilliant - though in his own way - man beside him.

These men are famous, made so by their father, their creator, but never make to flaunt it or shut down their fans. And this girl is no exception, having loved them since they first strolled into her life. The mere thought of them means everything to this girl, considering they have been there for her every last time she needed and expected them. She was never late, and neither were they. Not once....

Nine-year-old Rachel closes the book with a final smile at the glossy picture of Sir Arthur Conan Doyle.

"Thank you, Holmes," she whispers, stroking the cover of her favourite copy of The Adventures of Sherlock Holmes. "You too, Watson."

She bids her friends farewell and walks from her bedroom with a look of contentment still present upon her features. She is no longer saddened by the harsh words of the nasty students at school. Because she has her best friends, Sherlock Holmes and Dr. John Watson, and hey have given her an escape. A place of her own at 221B Baker Street. A place where Rachel can feel safe and untouchable to the bitches and bullies who can't reach her. Their parents have not even been conceived yet, let alone themselves.

She is happy here.

It is her own private sanctuary.

And, here, it is always 1895.

7.

Beehive by floppybelly.tumblr.com

John longed to scratch his side. He squirmed uncomfortably as the itch nagged at him, almost as though it knew he couldn't get to it through the thick-hided beekeeping suit. "Aren't you almost done, Sherlock? I can't believe you're doing this."

Sherlock withdrew his head from the giant beehive, the last in a line of five. "Yes, that should do it. Now I just need to run these samples against the one found on the victim. Let's go." Sherlock immediately started making towards the rental car, leaving John struggling with his suit and trying to apologize to the beekeeper.

"Hold up," he called to the impatient detective, "Some people actually use the equipment designed for this job. We're not all miraculous bee-whisperers, you know!"

Sherlock only laughed as he leaned against the car, suckling the raw honey from his fingers.

8.

Sir Arthur Conan Doyle by reichenbachtrip.tumblr.com

Sir Arthur Conan Doyle once mentioned to Joseph Bell, "Holmes is as inhuman as a Babbage's calculating machine and just about as likely to fall in love". There are many times in many portrayals in adaptations when Sherlock Holmes finds himself with a romantic interest, but in the original canon he tells Watson that he has never loved. To most, Sherlock Holmes is an example of a great detective and a man with the ability to remove himself from his feelings when he requires, but to others – including myself – Sherlock Holmes is an asexual and aromantic man who is both confident enough in who he is to not care about it, and is able to chase after his passions even more so than other people do.

9.

The Shaping of SH by on-the-side-of-the-angels.tumblr.com

When Sherlock Holmes was five, he was introduced to people other than his family. Mycroft, who was twelve then, already shined on every important meeting, gladly talking about school, life and his personal achievements. Sherlock wasn't as cooperative as his brother and, being only five years old, he soon complained his way out of every official dinner possible. It wasn't much use keeping him there anyways, the only thing the boy ever did was repeating 'dull' over and over again or exposing lies that were made in purpose of obligatory flattery. That way, instead of wasting his time at the dinner table with boring adults and his older brother, he could master the art of reading, difficult for every five year old boy, no matter how brilliant.

When Sherlock was ten, he could no longer escape all the horribly dull dinners held at his house. He was a big boy now, going to school and shining like a little star, so he couldn't hide away in his room anymore. Sherlock tried to scream 'dull' once or twice, but Mycroft, being the perfect teenager that he was, silenced him in an instant. Sherlock got very angry at him, but later they made a deal- Sherlock would act like a normal, perfect little boy and later Mycroft gave him his cool books from school to read. And, to be quite honest, even without the Holmes' brothers' deal, dinners weren't the most problematic. What Sherlock hated most was school, his boring classmates and under qualified teachers.

When Sherlock was fifteen, things haven't changed much. His life consisted of books, experiments and occasional insults (or objects) thrown at him. He didn't care much, though, for he was far better educated than they ever had a chance to be. Besides, it's not like he showed up at school every day. Once his teenage angst had set in, so did his rebellious attitude. Discouraged by the stupidity of the school staff and students, he mostly skipped class and examined birds and insects in the nearby park. If he got very lucky, he found a dead bird- they were a treat for the boy, art of decomposing at its finest. Sometimes he was brought to school almost by force- he spent his hours there sulking and mumbling insults at everybody. Except for one physics teacher, who took the boy under his wing and showed him the wonders of science. It still wasn't enough to bring Sherlock to school on a regular basis, but the boy surely was grateful for the man's attention, even if he never expressed his gratitude.

When Sherlock was twenty, he was already in college. He could be studying whatever, it didn't matter- he already knew most of what any professor could tell him and even if he didn't, he had books for a reason. But he went there anyway, mostly to make mommy happy. Additionally, he chose to get a degree in Physics, to annoy his brother, who couldn't stand their parents being so happy with their little son, all grown up and responsible and getting a real degree, unlike Mycroft's, who chose Art History. Although most of his classes were boring at best, the equipment his school provided was enough to keep Sherlock happy and not insulting his classmates more than the acceptable amount.

When Sherlock was twenty-five, he was out of college and out of his mind. The dullness of his previous life was nothing compared to the experience he got after he finished his education. Every job he tried was horribly boring, people were more than irritating and soon Sherlock couldn't stand to see anybody besides his family, but even his relatives' visits were severely restricted. Sherlock could go for days without speaking to anybody, he hardly ate and hardly slept, spending his time reading books and looking for other publications, the ones he hadn't read yet. But it couldn't last forever, so Sherlock went to look for his own thrill, a thrill to take away the dull ache of life. Life without job, without adventure, without stimulus. It didn't take him long to experience drugs and alcohol. The intoxication had him feeling extremely odd, yet he quickly got hooked. He expected himself to hate the lightheadedness and unclear mind that drugs and alcohol induced, but he didn't. Finally, there was something to stop this train of thoughts that was beeping constantly in his head. And even though Sherlock realized that it wasn't a gentle stop, but more a concrete wall the train has crashed into, he didn't care. His life was dull and boring, but at least he wasn't conscious enough to really feel it.

When Sherlock was 30, he was already out of rehab and on his two feet. He was working for Lestrade, who had pretty much saved him, sleeping and eating occasionally and trying his best not to overdose again. His reasons were trivial- he didn't want to see the disapproving look on his brother's face once more. Sherlock really tried to make the job for Lestrade everything that he needed, but it wasn't enough. He tried to dig up cold cases and solve them, tried out many experiments, tried to do anything, anything, to stop being bored but nothing was ever enough. But Sherlock pushed through, not entirely sure what for.

But now Sherlock is thirty-five and he knows exactly what for. It's been some time already that he found a new flat mate, John Watson, who then proceeded to accompany him on cases and write a blog about the two of them. John buys milk, arranges meetings with Mrs Hudson, cooks dinner sometimes or simply reminds Sherlock to eat, makes great tea, handles Mycroft and Anderson and is there every time Sherlock needs a text to be sent. But most importantly, John is a friend. The missing link between Sherlock and the world, between his brilliant mind and harsh reality.

10.
Who is Sherlock Holmes?
Authored by Sylvia Yi

"Who is Sherlock Holmes?" a young dapper fellow asked his mate at Scotland Yard. He was rather new to the whole police business and had heard a great deal of whispers about this famous man.

His partner scoffed. "Only the closest thing man kind has ever seen to a machine," he responded. "The man is brilliant, but he doesn't have to be so...so cold. I tried to greet him once and all I received was a curt nod. He calls himself a consulting detective, so i suppose that's what his official title would be."

The young man leaned towards the window, attempting to catch a glimpse of the aforementioned man out in the courtyard. "Who's the fellow walking beside him and Inspector Lestrade?" he inquired.

"Who?" his friend asked, following suit. "Oh, that must be that doctor Mr. Holmes met a few months ago. He tags along whenever Mr. Holmes assists with a case. I heard some men talking about him. Apparently, he used to be in the army and the last place he fought was in Afghanistan, I believe."

In a way, he envied the two men. They had received the opportunity to work with DI Lestrade, someone he saw as a role model of some sort in the police force. He had always read the articles Lestrade and Holmes appeared in in the newspaper and had become fascinated with solving crime which prompted him to become an officer of the law. He glanced back out the window and saw that the three men had disappeared.

"Quick. Act like you're busy," he said, scrambling to create the pretense that he had not just been slacking off a moment before. DI Lestrade strode down the hallway and around the corner towards the two new recruits.

"Good morning, officers," Lestrade politely greeted them.

"Good morning, Inspector," they promptly responded. Not far behind, Sherlock Holmes and the doctor came trailing in. Sherlock gave them a curt nod, barely glancing at the two men, but the doctor fellow stopped in front of them.

He held out his hand to shake theirs. "Good morning," he warmly greeted. The two recruits stood in awe as Sherlock Holmes had stopped to stand next to the doctor, silently waiting him to finish his salutations.

"Oh yes, gentlemen. This here is Mr.Sherlock Holmes," Lestrade gestured towards the tall, lean man with dark hair. "And this here, is Dr. John H. Watson," he gestured towards the shorter, stouter man. The two looked liked complete opposites, but were quite fetching in their own ways. "These two here are the newly appointed recruits I spoke to you about earlier, Officers Brixton and Wingham. I expect the lot of you to get along with one another as Holmes and Watson here will be assisting in the Danbury case."

"I already know what there is to know about them, Lestrade. No need for introductions," Holmes piped up from behind the doctor. "You, Officer Brixton: age approximate of twenty five years. Single. Went to a prestigious university before deciding to become an officer. You recently quit smoking, but started up again, presumably due to the pressures of the job from which one can assume you have rather fragile nerves which would be a bit of a hindrance out in the field. You—"

"Not now, Sherlock. Come," Dr. Watson interrupted, shooing Sherlock down the hall. "Goodbye, gentlemen. It was nice to meet you," he said as almost as an afterthought. He promptly turned his back on the two young men whose eyes widened in surprise.

"Must you do that every time?" Watson inquired of Sherlock.

"Force of habit, my dear friend," he replied simply, their voices trailing off as they walked farther down the hall.

"I told you he was brilliant," Wingham said.

"That fellow, Dr. Watson, must be some man to have the power to quiet the great Sherlock Holmes," Brixton added, still staring down the hall at the retreating figures.

11.
(Domestic Life at 221b) Morning Concerto
Hannah Rogers

3:15 am. Doctor John Hamish Watson blinked.

Still 3:15. The sun stubbornly remained somewhere beyond the London skyline, refusing to intervene in this struggle. His alarm of classic music twittered away to itself. One last try.

Blink.

3:16.

Damn surgery hours.

Stifling a yawn, John sat up, his sleep addled hand repeatedly missing the alarm. It was only when the fine violin solo was temporarily replaced with the scratching of pencil on paper that John remembered.

Sherlock Holmes was the pre-emptive alarm clock.

Fine, John though. Just what I need, strong cup of coffee and a good shout. Slipping on slippers which had chased murderers alongside the Thames and a dressing gown which had graced the halls of Parliament, John Watson went to yell at his flatmate for noise pollution. He descended stairs, forgetting to avoid the creaky step which would alert Sherlock to his approach. In the brief moment of natural silence, John realised something else.
Sherlock Holmes often played violin. He rarely played badly.
John hovered at the door, letting a thin slice of candlelight leave a scar across his eye. Sherlock never remembered to use electric lights: which was a blessing on the wallet. Mrs Hudson always lit them when it got late; hoping they would be therapeutic, though the fact they were burning was more a sign of chaos than anything

else. Sherlock was perched at the window, like a magpie awaiting an open chance to steal silver from the cutlery drawer. He held the violin at an alarming angle, plucking at the strings tentatively.

The air was thicker, the way it always was when Sherlock tried to a sneak a cigarette before changing his mind and throwing it into the fire. (It now shrivelled up among the coals, enveloping the room in smoke, akin to dragon with its tail wrapped around the detective's shoulders.) It was no question as to whether he would take notice of John's presence: the leg of Sherlock's trousers could have caught alight and it would doubtful as to whether he would raise an eyebrow. All that mattered was the notes, and the tangled mess they laid in.

Creeping back upstairs, John listened intently to their course. He had heard it many times and knew their path well. Sherlock has once commented how musical notes were similar to facts: played in any one of infinite orders, they could mean infinite things. Only one melody among the hundreds would be the proud work of the composer: and in facts this melody would be considered the truth. Even as the notes became sharper and the melody picked up tempo, John had already sorted his hair and tied his shoes. A dull thud followed: anyone else would have assumed it was the violin thrown aside, but Sherlock Holmes valued the state of instrument almost higher than his own life. It was the familiar sound of the World's Only Consulting Detective toppling over his coffee table.

"John!" Came the cry, cracked and rusty from days without use. "The game is afoot!"

Pictures, in order:

1. By actualginger.tumblr.com
2. "Art Nouveau Sherlock Blue" by nero749.deviantart.com
3. "Autobiography" by Kade
4. By cctheo.tumblr.com
5. "Chimpanzee Sherlock" by hedvig
6. By ea-love.tumblr.com
7. By ea-love.tumblr.com
8. By geothebio.tumblr.com
9. By hjat.tumblr.com
10. "Holmes" by Lotta Lundin
11. "Holmes" by mlysza.tumblr.com
12. "Holmes" by yourresidentginger.tumblr.com
13. By jas-tham.tumblr.com
14. By keep-the-macrame-secret.tumblr.com
15. By lightjirachi97.tumblr.com
16. By machomachi.tumblr.com
17. By potterwholock.tumblr.com
18. By reapersun.tumblr.com
19. "Save Undershaw" by Maria Fleischhack
20. "Sherlock" by elocinaqui.deviantart.com
21. "Sherlock Holmes" by Hannah Rubery (dreamingphyscopath.tumblr.com)
22. "Stippling" by cumbercrieff.tumblr.com
23. By soptfeedingme.tumblr.com
24. "Thinking" by kaylanorail.tumblr.com
25. By wonderfulworldofme.tumblr.com

WHEN
THE
NO
IT MIGHT
MUST

Sherlock Holmes

IN THE YEAR 1878 I TOOK MY DEGREE OF DOCTOR of Medicine of the University of London, and proceeded to Netley to go through the course prescribed for surgeons in the Army • We met next day, as he had arranged, and inspected the rooms at No. 221b, Baker Street • "Get your hat," he said. "You wish me to come?" "Yes, if you have nothing better to do." • Sherlock Holmes and I looked blankly at each other and then burst simultaneously into an uncontrollable fit of laughter • "But love is an emotional thing, and whatever is emotional is opposed to that true cold reason which I place above all things." • "You see, but you do not observe. The distinction is clear." • Holmes was for the moment as startled as I. His hand closed like a vise upon my wrist in his agitation • The very intimate relations which had existed between Holmes and myself became to some extent modified • "I think you know me well enough, Watson, to understand that I am by no means a nervous man. At the same time, it is stupidity rather than courage to refuse to recognise danger when it is close upon you." • "You have probably never heard of Professor Moriarty?" said he • It was the

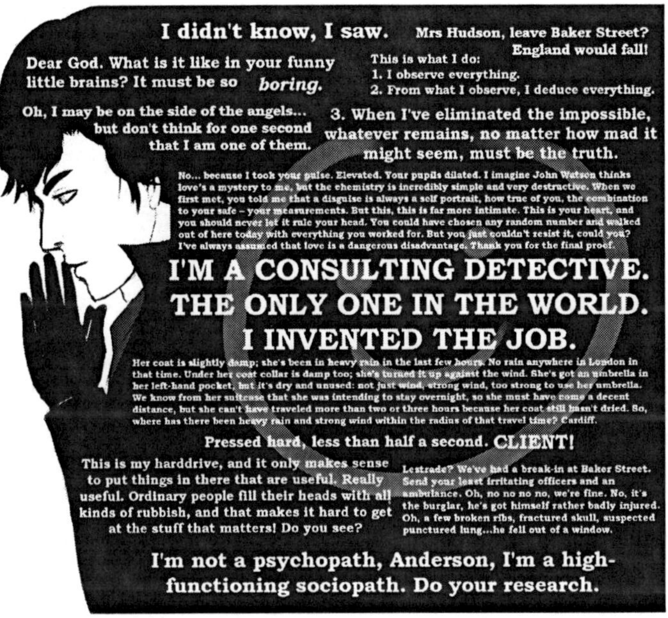

I didn't know, I saw.

Mrs Hudson, leave Baker Street?
England would fall!

Dear God. What is it like in your funny
little brains? It must be so *boring.*

This is what I do:
1. I observe everything.
2. From what I observe, I deduce everything.

Oh, I may be on the side of the angels...
but don't think for one second
that I am one of them.

3. When I've eliminated the impossible,
whatever remains, no matter how mad it
might seem, must be the truth.

No... because I took your pulse. Elevated. Your pupils dilated. I imagine John Watson thinks
love's a mystery to me, but the chemistry is incredibly simple and very destructive. When we
first met, you told me that a disguise is always a self portrait, how true of you, the combination
to your safe – your measurements. But this, this is far more intimate. This is your heart, and
you should never let it rule your head. You could have chosen any random number and walked
out of here today with everything you worked for. But you just couldn't resist it, could you?
I've always assumed that love is a dangerous disadvantage. Thank you for the final proof.

I'M A CONSULTING DETECTIVE.
THE ONLY ONE IN THE WORLD.
I INVENTED THE JOB.

Her coat is slightly damp; she's been in heavy rain in the last few hours. No rain anywhere in London in
that time. Under her coat collar is damp too; she's turned it up against the wind. She's got an umbrella in
her left-hand pocket, but it's dry and unused: not just wind, strong wind, too strong to use her umbrella.
We know from her suitcase that she was intending to stay overnight, so she must have come a decent
distance, but she can't have traveled more than two or three hours because her coat still hasn't dried. So,
where has there been heavy rain and strong wind within the radius of that travel time? Cardiff.

Pressed hard, less than half a second. CLIENT!

This is my harddrive, and it only makes sense
to put things in there that are useful. Really
useful. Ordinary people fill their heads with all
kinds of rubbish, and that makes it hard to get
at the stuff that matters! Do you see?

Lestrade? We've had a break-in at Baker Street.
Send your least irritating officers and an
ambulance. Oh, no no no no, we're fine. No, it's
the burglar, he's got himself rather badly injured.
Oh, a few broken ribs, fractured skull, suspected
punctured lung...he fell out of a window.

I'm not a psychopath, Anderson, I'm a high-
functioning sociopath. Do your research.

HEDVIG U.
JAN 2012

I may be on the
side of the angels

«I am a consulting detective.
The only one in the world,
I invented the job.»

SHERL CKS
MIND PALACE
NO ANDERSONS ALLOWED
I ♥ JOHN

HOLMES

Sherlock
Holmes

In height he was rather over six feet and so excessively lean that he seemed considerably taller...
His eyes were sharp and piercing...
His thin hawk-like nose gave his whole expression an air of alertness and decision...
His chin, too, had the prominence and squareness which mark the man of determination...
His hands were invariably blotted with ink and stained with chemicals, yet he was possessed of extraordinary delicacy of touch...

Sherlock
Holmes

Macho
Machi

alone is
what i
have
alone protects me.

Diary of John Watson - 221B Baker Street
The Adventures

Come
If Convenient.
If not Come Anyway.
I'm a High Functioning
Caring Sociopath. BORED!
I'm fine
is not an advantage.
Catch...you...later. Lestrade
I NEED A CASE! John
I'm afraid. Thank you.
I'm fine. Mrs Hudson.
I don't have friends.
Just one. Take
I'm fine
my hand!
Alone
protects me.
Goodbye
John.
I'm not
okay.

SHERLOCK HOLMES

UW 2012

Poetry

1.

***Human* By myownturku.tumblr.com**

human.

can one be so tired
that in my sleep
did I not move, or
am I in psychosis
maybe analyzed myself
wrong
couldn't believe, eerie
haunting, as if
the nightmares of you
swept through my chest
I toss and turn
in my bed
because you have ripped
my heart instead
I do believe in you,
so there.
Sherlock Holmes,
just don't be
dead

2.

The Fall By sherlockedandnotginger.tumblr.com

He asked if you would do this for him,
But what is your battle now?
It is to turn your grief loose.
It is to feel the slackness of your limbs
as you fall to the pavement
beside his bloodied body.
It is to count the seconds between each breath,
remembering the stream of his voice declaring disdain
for the predictability of the world.
It is enduring the emptiness of his chair,
the silence of his violin falling out of tune,
the insidious creeping nothingness of your days,
no longer filled with his chaos and colour.
It is ignoring the cup of tea you've made for him out of habit.
It is in the stacks of books that you cannot sell,
because his name is scrawled,
possessive and disdainful on each flyleaf.
It's a splash of yellow spray paint on the wall,
A merry smile shot dead,
showing you that you must bear
this inane and manic world
alone.

3.

Domestic Life at 221b by sothisonetime1.tumblr.com

One o'clock in the morning,
Gun fire hits the darkness,
Street lamps salute the winding street ways
On which 221b stands before us.

As sunlight hits the window sills,
The morning begins to flutter,
A small old lady in a frail night gown,
Soon will start to mutter.

She runs around the disaster sight,
Handing out tea cups and spoon's,
"Sherlock Holmes this has too stop"
She shout's as she leaves the room.

Confused and wanting answers,
John Watson bursts into the room,
Stares deeply into Sherlock's eyes
Knowing there's work for them to do.

And now as he sits in his arm chair,
Blank expression on his face,
Sherlock Holmes consulting detective,
ready to solve another case.

4.

By Gun and Fall by mycroft-broke-my-action-man.tumblr.com

Great games are played, great minds at war,

But only one side the people saw,

The story was a lie smothered in truth,

One a great criminal, the other a grand sleuth,

Criminal by gun and sleuth by fall,

The doctor is left with no one at all,

Alone with a limp, exist in shades of grey,

Words of freedom he never can say,

But what he did was a request so sincere,

One last miracle, for the sleuth to appear,

But three more years our dear doctor must wait, Before Sherlock Holmes will call at his gate.

-Alys Messenger

It seems their choice but it's far from so,

5.

"A Study in Yellow" by murf1307.tumblr.com

We'll run, we'll run
Bandanas to the wind
For the man, the man we believe in.

Paint our eyes yellow,
Paint our eyes yellow
For the man we believe in.

Smiley faces, IOUs,
Because the devil wears Westwood
And we won't let the lie stand.

Paint our eyes yellow,
Paint our eyes yellow,
For the man we believe in.

We'll blind our eyes to the lie
With the colour yellow;
One yellow slash
For the man we believe in.

6.

A Poem About a Certain Flat by Mackenzee "Muse" Borges

It is a home
For large intellect and heart
It is a home,
A work of art.

Adorned with skulls
And musical yaks.
It's filled with tea
And deerstalker hats.

The sound of violin
Is in the air.
And blogging is done
Very much in there.

Head in the fridge
A microwaved ear;
All the experiments
Are done in here.

There's never milk
Or food in general.
It's alright
They eat at Angelo's.

It's a place for rest
A place for thought,
And on the wall

A smiley face gets shot.

It's watched by snipers
Dominatrix, and police.
And yet the darn thing's
Still on a lease.

Two men live there,
One large, one small.
The little one's got heart,
The brains are with the tall.

But they love their home,
Their land-lady too.
And without it there's no place
That could contain the two.

It's got an address;
Yes, only one.
It's 221b Baker Street,
Westminster 1.

7.

Linear Regression by chenra.tumblr.com/ chen63.deviantart

Sit and tell a story, John.
Bring a detective novel and a thermos of tea)two cups(
read it and present it to the judging gravestone
it listens with an ugly sneer
and scoffs at the dialogue
)though he's dead
you can hear his voice(
and you've never heard a silence so wretched
)he demanded it in life;
he would not receive it, even in death,
so help him God(

Bring along an encyclopedia of poisons
list them off to the name engraved
)the man engraved also,
for he himself could never be entombed(
You'll consider them
what they might taste like on your tongue
)probably like dust – as everything else
does(
Consider the impossible things to say
(I you)
or to sign
(you I)
or to symbol
(≠ Σ(=?); ÷ ♥);
the arithmetic ends
with a newly-stained entry for

hemlock

You're beginning to break down, John

)fairy tales
are for little children
the ones you see in your office, sick, sad, snotty

why couldn't the book have stayed closed?(

Carry your cane if you must, John
if the pain won't stay in your heart

toxins will leak, and all barriers have weak spots
)even in a heart hidden in a well of earth and stone and ice and —
and bound by a scarf that's made of midnight(

tell it through to the end, John,
a gravestone doesn't go anywhere.

9.

An Angel's Fall by Jessica Carducci

Blood almost black against the ground
slowly pooling beneath him.
Splashed and smeared across cement
by approaching feet
rushing to aid the fallen hero.

He's lying there
and now I'm down too.
Face pressed into the asphalt
ears ringing
needing to move.

They don't want to let me
to let me see him.
But I'm his doctor.
His friend.
He needs me.

I see his face now.
It's the same face but not at all.
The pale, hard angles are still his
but the cold beauty is transcendent.
Gaze focused on a plane I cannot see.

I can touch him now
check for life
look for a pulse.
But there is nothing to find.
I am alone once again.

10.

I Believe in Sherlock Holmes by sherlypuff.tumblr

Moriarty was real.
And Moran he cries.
His tears they fall down.
His tears turns to ice.
John in a chair.
Waiting for him.
The one with the deerstalker.
The one who is dead.
While he sits in his chair,
he thinks for himself
"I belive in Sherlock Holmes."

11.

I Dream of It Every Night by dis-combobulate.tumblr.com

The exact texture of your cold
wrist mottled with blood
clings to my fingertips

I dream of it every night

The way your vocal chords
Normally striking like a cello
resonated distortedly through the phone

I dream of it every night

The way the street drowned
with the roaring of blood in my ears:
My senses consumed by your descending body

I dream of it

every

fucking

night

God the way your hair slid
through the blood like processed meat
and how the moment I touched you
I knew you weren't him
not anymore no you were a corpse
not as bloated and sand-grit and flayed into pieces
as I'm used to dreaming of
but you weren't-

you were dead

just dead

I dream of it every night

and I used to furl up
on top of the newly turned earth
my bones over yours
and my bones over yours
and my bones over yours
I think you are burned into
the backs of my eyelids
and the nerves on my fingertips and
sticking sickly sweet inside my nostrils

(I dream of you every night)

12.

Not So Different by Catherine Benham

We're not so different, he and I,
One a healer, one a spy,
One an assassin, a hunter by trade,
The other a doctor, deliverer of aid.

Both in the service of country and Queen,
Sent home by a bullet and scandal unseen,
Both returned home with wounded pride,
Seeking new purpose, this Jekyll and Hyde.

He made an acquaintance, a man of repute,
Whose intelligent workings I cannot dispute.
They formed an alliance, unlikely but strong,
At his side he had hope of a place to belong.

My sharp-shooting talents had not been ignored,
Soldier turned mercenary; trust, my reward.
A chance at a glimpse into London's great mind,
This criminal maestro, this one of a kind.

A shadowy game between the two,
Schemes were plotted and foiled anew,
And all the while we lay in wait,
To clean up the mess they were bound to create.

Miles were travelled to lead us to here,
This wide-open landscape, this valley of fear,

We watched as he sauntered, so devil-may-care,
But all of us sensed there was death in the air.

I was ordered to wait, concealed in a nook,
So there I remained above that rich brook.
But the doctor retreated, still kept in the dark,
Denied the duty of playing his part.

Thoughts of failure never entered my head,
As I witnessed them fall, my gut filled with dread.
Then to see that wretch crawl up from the edge,
My blood did boil and I swore this pledge:

For as long as I lived, I would track this man down,
Not a care for his talents or worthy renown.
Then I spied as he fled the dear doctor's return,
And was struck by his sorrow, a sickening burn.

I wondered right then, if he were me,
The lengths he would go to to make the pain flee.
Would he punish the villain and undo the good?
In seeing his grief I believe that he would.
The pain that he feels is akin to my own,
But the tears that he sheds are but his alone.

Both in the shadows of two great men,
One armed with a rifle, the other a pen,
Tools to avenge the ones they once served,
Yet only the one is justly deserved.
We're not so different, he and I,
Both are mourners, one is a lie.

13.

Valentine by *Unknown*

Roses are red,
Violets are blue.
Is your name Reichenbach?
Because I'm falling for you!

14.
Amicae Antiquae by Maggie Cason

She is the eerie, preceding calm and he is the violent storm.
She brings life and he, death.
She is impossibly old and enduring while he is far too young and fleeting.
She is the earth and he is the swift wind.
She is the velvet blackness of deep space that provides a backdrop for his blazing supernova that dulls every other star by comparison.

They fill the roles of Queen and loyal steward, of aging mother and adult son.

He knows every twist and dip of her streets, has memorized nearly every feature of her architecture.

She watches him dash after the solutions to his puzzles, purge her of constant impurities created by his own kind.

They are companions, friends, they are opposing and synonymous forces.

She is stability and he is change.

She is London and he is Sherlock Holmes.

15.

SHERLOCK

By "Sherly Waffles"

Sherlock is great
Sherlock has the key to every gate
Sherlock is clever
No one is better
Sherlock is an arrogant ass
And sure nothing less
But his heart is growing
And his temper is slowing
He knows things you can't comprehend
But will you to the evil send
He's lost without John
Who helps him to move on
John is full of thrust
And can easily take Sherlock's outburst
John is his only friend
And he stays with Sherlock till the end
John and Sherlock aren't gay
Who thinks this, has to pay!
Molly loves Sherlock
And she shows this around the clock
Molly is shy and lovely
But Sherlock didn't see her clearly
Jim Moriarty is evil
He played with Molly which was cruel
Moriarty was real
To believe this isn't a big deal
He was Sherlock's arch enemy

And brought him to a fall
But this fall wasn't deadly
But Moriarty is dead surely
Sherlock is alive
And soon Moriarty will in hell arrive
John, don't cry!
Sherlock's death is just a lie
Calm down and carry on
You know Sherlock, John!
Anderson and Sally are so stupid
That's why they together fit
Lestrade isn't clever either
But not as stupid neither
Mrs Hudson lost one boy
He was her motherly toy
Mycroft is a bad brother
Who the favourite was of their mother
Everyone seems sad and cries
And thinks that under earth our hero lies
But Sherlock is alive!

<u>I BELIEVE IN</u>
<u>SHERLOCK</u>

17.

Who Watches the Watson? By Lesly Pollock/ chainsawmascara.tumblr.com

You watched him
Fifteen paces behind
Buying bread or a sweater,
Consulting Detectives don't resign.

The day you were following,
that day he bought rosin

You took lunch downstairs
just so you could listen
while cleverly disguised.

There was the evening he saw you outside -
convinced he was dreaming
drew the curtains to hide
from your memory.

The specter he'd always seek
of the man who made him feel alive.

And he watched Mrs. Hudson
the way you'd have wanted;
but Sherlock, when he wore your scarf -
that was the day it broke your heart.

18.

The Fall by christyrebecca.tumblr.com

I remember the day,
twas not long ago.
It changed my life,
and you will never know.

The feelings I felt,
the nightmares I had.
I don't blame you,
because it's not your bad.

I wonder what would happen,
if you were still here.
Would I punch you in the face,
or hug you in tears.

I am an army doctor,
my traumas are bad.
I've felt so much,
the amount of tears I've shed.

But that's nothing,
compared to that day.
I finally had a friend,
and you took that away.

I still believe in you,
no one will tell me otherwise.
You told me you were a fake,

but I know they're all lies.

So please stop it,
be alive instead.
Could you do that for me?
just don't be… dead.

19.

1895 by Sarah Mack

Sometimes we still sit in our chairs
Angled around the fireplace
The one we never light
(Excepting that one Christmas
When he was his terrible self, then
Surprisingly—
Apologized).

We don't say much
But I watch him out of the
Narrow of my eye, mesmerized.
If I turn toward his dark chair
He's gone.

I hid the cigarettes
Under the skull on the mantle.
Even now, I let them be
Hopelessly praying
He might take them down
Smoke them, curse his weakness.
I get up,
Leg aching something fierce.
I turn away
Go to the kitchen,
My best friend reappears
Guarding my back
Perched on the back

Of his black leather chair
Shoes on the seat cushion
His long pale fingers steepled
Brush soft against his lips
Skin between his brows creased.
Before him, I was so alone
After him, it's not so different
From before.

20.

The Reichenbach Fall by littleredhatter.deviantart

Together they fell
Through the dark abyss
Of heaven and hell

Rivers of red
Rivers of blue
It was a great fall
I'm telling you

Tears of loss
Tears of sorrow
It made one man
Completely hollow

The Spider weaved his web
of hate and gore
And the Reichenbach hero
Was a hero no more

22.

The Brink of the Fall: Or, I Should Not Dream of Stirring Out Without You by AN

No matter how mad it may be
Once you eliminate the impossible
Whatever remains is the truth.

There's no credit left once you explain
The conjuror's trick has no magic, exposed
No matter how mad it must be

An exception disproves the rule
(You know my methods)
Whatever remains is the truth.

You see, but you do not observe:
One begins to twist facts to suit,
No matter how mad it must be

Life is infinitely stranger than anything we invent
So there is nothing more deceptive than an obvious fact
Whatever remains is the truth.

If you were dying, what would you say?
Goodbye? It is impossible as I state it -
No matter how mad it may be
Whatever remains is the truth.

———- By A.N. This villanelle is primarily comprised of quotes

23.

Sestina for a Last Lesson by 221b-bitchstreet.tumblr.com

Train yourself, no matter the distractions, to deduce
There is no magic, no mystery in the method
Only careful logic and resistance to the impossible
All men see, but step further and observe
Pick out the distractions, dissect the matter
And there's the way that you begin to trace the truth.

Not that they will thank you for the truth
In the end, they're pathetically simple to deduce
But then again, how much do tiny minds matter?
Ignore the jibes, the taunts, the disbelief, and it's a method
For passing by, above it all, show no disturbance they observe
Let them imagine your calm unbreakable, your heart impossible

The saying's wrong: some things are utterly impossible
Ignore them, and find the remaining probable the truth
There are no secrets from you, if you only observe
Everything, let nothing evade you, and from it, you deduce
Correctly, if you've been careful, if you've a perfect method
To what seems madness, remember, it must matter.

The work must be of consequence, your efforts matter
Otherwise, survival is suffocation, living impossible
How do dullards get along, what dreary method
Allows them to plod on? If only you could deduce
A way to quiet a racing mind – some nights, if truth
Be told, you envy that silence that you can only observe.

But then, only at the proper moment, here, observe
Cut through the fog and unearth the hidden matter
Like a rabbit from a hat, and show what genius may deduce
It seems so simple to them, after, a most obvious truth
Plucked from a puzzle, previously impervious, impossible
Made child's play by the precision of your method.

Never waver, never falter, hold to the method
Eyes open, mind working, perceive, process, observe
Eradicate all doubt; show all that remains is truth
For next to truth, nothing else can ever matter
To imagine otherwise - impossible
Let nothing limit what you're willing to deduce.

And here, you have the Method - make it matter,
Remember me and observe, forgetting is impossible
Deduce the things I never said, and hear all my unspoken truth

Links

Royalties from The Art of Deduction go to Help For Heroes.

www.helpforheroes.org.uk

The book also aims to raise awareness for Save Undershaw – the campaign to save and restore Sir Arthur Conan Doyle's former home. Undershaw is where he brought Sherlock Holmes back to life, and should be preserved for future generations of Holmes fans.

Save Undershaw www.saveundershaw.com

Facebook www.facebook.com/saveundershaw

You can read more about Sir Arthur Conan Doyle and Undershaw in Alistair Duncan's book (share of royalties to the Undershaw Preservation Trust) – An Entirely New Country and in the amazing compilation Sherlock's Home – The Empty House (all royalties to the Trust).

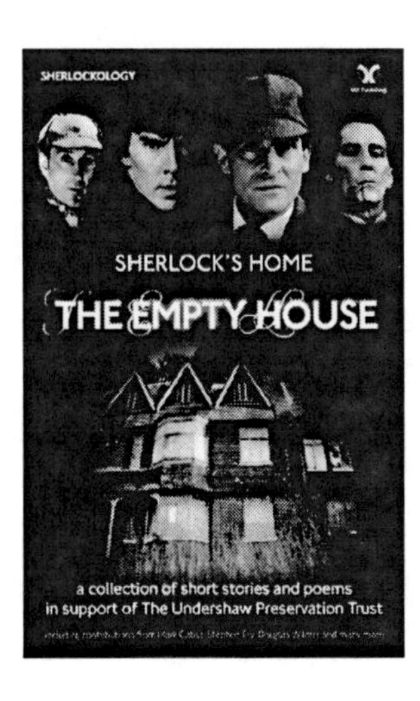

From one of the world's largest Sherlock Holmes publishers dozens of new novels and books from the top Holmes authors –

including Alistair Duncan, winner of the 2011 Howlett Literary Award (Sherlock Holmes book of the year) for
'The Norwood Author'

www.mxpublishing.com

New in 2012 [Novels unless stated]:
Sherlock Holmes and the Plague of Dracula
Sherlock Holmes and The Adventure of The Jacobite Rose [Play]
Sherlock Holmes and The Whitechapel Vampire
Holmes Sweet Holmes
The Detective and The Woman: A Novel of Sherlock Holmes
Sherlock Holmes Tales From The Stranger's Room
The Sherlock Holmes Who's Who [Reference]
Sherlock Holmes and The Dead Boer at Scotney Castle
The Secret Journal of Dr Watson
A Professor Reflects on Sherlock Holmes [Essay Collection]
Sherlock Holmes of The Lyme Regis Legacy
Sherlock Holmes and The Discarded Cigarette [Short Novel]
Sherlock Holmes On The Air [Radio Plays]
Sherlock Holmes and The Murder at Lodore Falls
Untold Adventure of Sherlock Holmes
Sherlock Holmes and The Terrible Secret
Sherlock Holmes and The Element of Surprise
Sherlock Holmes and The Edinburgh Haunting
The Hound of The Baskervilles [Play]
56 Sherlock Holmes Stories in 56 Days [Reviews]
The Many Watsons [Reviews]
The 1895 Murder

Also from MX Publishing

Sherlock Holmes Travel Guides

London Devon

In e-book an interactive guide to London

400 locations linked to Google Street View.

Also from MX Publishing

Cross over fiction featuring great villains from history

Fantasy Sherlock Holmes

Also from MX Publishing

Sherlock Holmes and Young Winston Trilogy

Book 1 – The Deadwood Stage
Book 2 – The Jubilee Plot
Book 3 – The Giant Moles

"An inspired notion to introduce a young Winston Churchill into the lives of Holmes and Watson and fortunately the inspired writing lives up to that inspired notion. Everything about this book, whether it be plot, casting, characters or dialogue is spot on. Mr Hogan, quite simply, does not put a foot wrong with volume, roll on the next two!!"

The Baker Street Society

Also from MX Publishing

Carrying the seal of the Conan Doyle Estate.....

On the most secret and dangerous assignment of their lives, Sherlock Holmes and Dr. Watson are sent into the newborn Soviet Union to rescue The Romanovs: Nicholas and Alexandra and their innocent children. Will Holmes and Watson be able to change history? Will they even be able to survive?

Also from MX Publishing

A rare and charming children's book featuring Sherlock Holmes

CPSIA information can be obtained at www.ICGtesting.com
Printed in the USA
LVOW121553020513

332035LV00015B/654/P

9 781780 922348